Perhaps Briony should never have married Logan Adair. Her father had been violently opposed to the marriage; Logan himself had been dubious. But Briony loved him and had no doubts at all. Yet the marriage had been nothing but a farce from the very beginning. Shouldn't Briony cut her losses and admit defeat?

Books you will enjoy
by SARA CRAVEN

FLAME OF DIABLO

It was imperative that Rachel should go off to Columbia to find her brother, who was searching for a treasure of emeralds—but her only chance of success lay with Vitas de Mendoza. He agreed to help her—but at a price. Would she find the price too high? Or would she pay it—far too willingly?

SOLITAIRE

Solitaire, her kindly Uncle Jim's house in the Vendée region of France, represented a welcoming haven after years of unhappiness—but Marty arrived there to find her uncle gone and in his place a hard, unwelcoming stranger—Luc Dumarais. There would be no haven at Solitaire now, she realised. And if she did not get away quickly, there would be even more unhappiness ... for Luc Dumarais was right out of her league.

MOTH TO THE FLAME

To help her selfish sister Jan to marry Mario Vallone, against the wishes of his stern brother Santino, Juliet pretended to be Jan. And all she got for her pains was to be whisked off to a lonely part of Calabria, with a man who had the lowest possible opinion of her—and whose attraction she was finding it increasingly hard to resist ...

HIGH TIDE AT MIDNIGHT

When the only relatives she had in the world made it plain that she was unwelcome in their house, Morwenna took herself defiantly off to some old friends of her mother's in Cornwall, hoping they would offer her a home. She had gone there to ask a favour, but as things turned out she remained to bestow one—but at the expense of all her peace of mind.

FUGITIVE WIFE

BY

SARA CRAVEN

MILLS & BOON LIMITED
LONDON W1

First published 1980
Australian copyright 1980
Philippine copyright 1980
This edition 1980

ISBN 0 263 73286 X

Set in Linotype Pilgrim 10 on 11½ pt.

Made and printed in Great Britain by
Richard Clay (The Chaucer Press), Ltd., Bungay, Suffolk

CHAPTER ONE

THE track was too steep and stony for the car, so she parked it at the bottom, just off the village road, and walked the rest of the way, the heels of her elegant boots sliding a little on the uneven surface.

She was hurrying, almost running, and deliberately she made herself slow down because the last thing she wanted to risk in this isolated spot was a sprained ankle.

She rounded the slight bend in the track, pausing to catch her breath and shift her suitcase to her other hand, and saw the cottage up ahead of her looking small and rather squat. The full force of the wind caught her, penetrating the thickness of her sheepskin coat as easily as if it was a chiffon veil. 'A lazy wind,' Aunt Hes had always called it. 'Too idle to go round, so it goes straight through you instead.'

It was degrees colder here. It had been quite a pleasant late autumn day when she had left London, with a misty sun shining through the bare branches of the trees, and an invigorating nip in the air. But the further north she had driven, the greyer the skies had become. And here they were slate-dark and threatening over Kirkby Fell, and almost close enough to touch, she thought with a shiver.

It would be good to get inside and get warm. That was, if there was any fuel in the cottage. She wished she had been able to contact Mrs Barnes in the village who kept a friendly eye on the unoccupied house for Aunt Hes. She made sure there was fuel, and usually a stock of provisions for when Aunt Hes wanted to use the cottage. Or to lend it for a holiday retreat or a honeymoon ...

But she wouldn't think about that now. That was what she had come here to escape from. To forget about, if she could. Suddenly there had been this desperate need to evade all the pressures, both subtle and overt, which were being exerted.

And so she'd flung a few things into a case and driven away north without telling a soul where she was going. She'd not even been able to contact Aunt Hes and make sure she had no objections to her using the cottage, because this was the time of year that her aunt always visited friends in the South of France. And who could blame her? she thought as she mounted the last few yards of the track. No one in their right mind faced with a choice between November in the South of France or on the side of a North Yorkshire fell would choose the fell.

She had left a note at the London house stating simply that she was going away to think things out, and would everyone please leave her alone, and not try to find her or contact her. Seen in retrospect, it had been a melodramatic thing to do, an overreaction, she supposed, to the events of the past week. But wasn't she entitled to that, under the circumstances?

And no one would guess that she had come here—of all places. That was what had kept her going when other destinations had beckoned her from the road signs on the motorway. Destinations with no painful associations, where there would be people to talk to and things to see. Not an isolated cottage at the top of a cart track with only sheep for company.

She pushed open the small white gate in the low grey stone wall, and went in. The flower borders on each side of the narrow path were lank and overgrown with weeds which brushed her legs as she moved between them. The gate needed painting, she noticed, and so did the whole of the outside of the cottage. If the weather had been warmer, she might have tackled it; the physical effort of stripping down the woodwork and applying undercoat and gloss might have been just what she needed.

She'd said she'd come away to think, but wasn't it nearer the truth to say that she'd come to escape from her thoughts?

All that remained now was to find the key to the front door. She mentally crossed her fingers that Mrs Barnes had not removed it for safe-keeping, or Aunt Hes found a new and safer hidey-hole for it. But it was still there, where it had always been left, under the piece of broken paving stone to the right of the front door.

The door yielded under her hand with a slight protesting squeak, and she went in, closing it behind her and leaning against it while her breathing steadied, feeling oddly like a small animal which had reached its refuge just ahead of the hunters.

She closed her eyes and let the silence surround her, and gradually the small sounds of the cottage and its environs began to impinge on her consciousness—the rustling and stirrings of the ancient fabric of the building itself, the whine of the rising wind in the eaves, the harsh calling of rooks from the fields behind, the distant bleat of a sheep, and nearer at hand the slow reassuring beat of the bracket clock which occupied pride of place on the overmantel of the room Aunt Hes always insisted on calling the parlour. The air smelt faintly musty, but it was only the inevitable odour of a house which had been shut up and untenanted. There was no tell-tale smell of damp or dry rot. Mrs Barnes did her job well, she thought. The place was regularly aired and warmed.

Briony opened her eyes and glanced round. There was a small flurry of envelopes just inside the door and she bent and picked them up. Mostly circulars by the look of things, she thought, tossing them negligently on to the hallstand. She left her case at the foot of the narrow stairs and walked into the living room.

Mrs Barnes did her job not just well, but superlatively, she thought appreciatively as her eyes fell on the fire laid ready in the grate, with the filled coal bucket, and the wicker basket full of sweet-smelling logs all to hand. It was almost as if she was expected. But that was silly. The impulse which had driven her here had not permitted any advance warning. No one knew where she was. No one at all.

No one, she repeated soundlessly, and her hands met in front of her, gripping each other with an odd painful intensity so that her rings bit into her flesh. She looked down wincing, and saw the flat gleam of the plain gold band on her left hand. She dragged it over her knuckle and threw it across the room with all her might. She heard the tinkle as it landed and rolled on the flagged floor. But she did not see where it went, and she did not want to see.

'I'm Briony Trevor,' she told herself fiercely. 'Briony Adair never existed. Never. And nothing that's happened makes the slightest difference to that.'

A tiny lean-to scullery opened off the living room, and she went through to make sure there was water, and that the electricity supply was switched on. Even if it wasn't, she could manage for one night, she thought. She knew where Aunt Hes kept the candles, and a small camping stove. But everything seemed to be in working order, and she filled the kettle, and set it to boil while she looked about her. There was a jar of instant coffee, which she sniffed dubiously, and some rather dusty-looking tea-bags in a brightly coloured caddy. Beggars could not be choosers, she thought, opting for probably nasty coffee, drunk black. Tomorrow she would go to the shop in the village and see about milk, and other provisions. But she would make do for tonight.

When she'd made her drink, she would light the fire, and see about airing some bedding.

The fire had been laid in the old-fashioned way, with spills of tightly rolled newspaper and kindling. It caught as soon as she put a match to it, and she knelt placing lumps of coal on the blazing edifice and watching the greedy tongues of flame licking round them.

She fetched her mug of coffee and sat on the high-backed wooden rocker close by the hearth to drink it.

She felt tired suddenly and drained as if this last small effort had finally exhausted her resources. She knew she ought to go upstairs to lie down, but it all seemed too much trouble. Presently she would find the bedding she needed. Presently. But for the moment it was enough to sit quietly with her hands clamped round the comforting warmth of the mug and feel the first tentative heat from the fire reaching out to her. She needed very badly to feel warm. There was a chill deep inside her.

But was this really the right place to come to dispel it? The coffee tasted suddenly bitter in her mouth and she set the mug down with a faint grimace. It had seemed a good idea. The ideal place to exorcise all her demons, to lay her ghosts to rest, she had thought. The only place, in fact. But now as darkness came crowding outside the small windows and the shadows gathered about her, she was not so sure any more.

She should get up and draw the curtains, and light the lamps—one on the square table by the window and the other in the book-lined recess beside the fireplace. But there was no hurry for that.

She was no longer a child to be frightened of the dark, she thought wryly. Her fears and hang-ups were all tangible now, and all to do with reality. Shadows could not hurt her, but people could, and had, and still might.

Sighing, she stretched her legs out in front of her. Slim-fitting trousers in grey cord covered her to her ankles, and a cream-coloured lambswool sweater with a high roll collar reached almost to her pointed chin. A broad-faced watch, its bracelet made of fine gold mesh, encircled her wrist. On her right hand a moonstone ring gleamed. Her left hand looked strangely bare without her wedding ring. Logan's ring.

She touched the mark on her marriage finger which showed where it had rested, her lips twisting slightly. Throwing it away had been a gesture, that was all. It had altered nothing. Legally, she was still Logan's wife, even though for months she had believed she was Logan's widow.

She lifted her hands and removed the two tortoiseshell combs which confined her shoulder-length copper hair behind her ears, shaking it loose around her face. She pressed her fingertips against her temples in an effort to relieve the slight tense ache which was beginning to build up there.

She bent forward and added another shovel of coal to the now brightly glowing fire, then leaned back, her eyes closed, trying to shut out the thoughts, the tantalising memories which buzzed and vibrated in her brain.

Logan standing in this very room, the usually cynical lines of his mouth relaxing into unexpected tenderness. His voice husky as he said 'Hello, wife,' and his arms reached for her.

At the time, she'd reckoned that to be the happiest moment of her life, happier than the actual wedding ceremony only a few hours before in London, because, then, in the register office, she'd been aware of her father's absence and of his continuing resentment of her marriage. But here in this room, alone with Logan, nothing else had seemed to matter. Her father's disapproval had seemed a long way away, and almost immaterial.

As Logan's arms had closed around her, and her lips had parted eagerly beneath his kiss, it had seemed that they would share this closeness for ever, that nothing or no one could ever separate them.

A mirthless smile curved her mouth. In retrospect, that conviction had a terrible irony.

She didn't want to look back now, to remember everything that had happened. Tomorrow, she thought, tomorrow when I'm less tired—more able to cope. But even as the thought formulated itself, she knew it was self-deception. So far she had signally failed to manage any aspect of her life. Wasn't that why she was here? Why she had fled to this little retreat in the wilds of Yorkshire, just to escape from a situation which she could neither control nor understand. She had come, telling herself that she had to think things out. This was the reason for her presence here. She could not, must not allow herself to escape again.

Besides, memories were pressing on her brain, presenting her with images, that she believed she had safely shut away for ever. No, her mind cried out in rebellion. I don't want to look back. I don't want the pain of it. In the past year she had made herself a tight safe cocoon where troubling memories could not pursue her. She had thought it was impregnable, but now she recognised that for the illusion it was. Where emotions were concerned, was anyone ever totally invulnerable, she wondered?

She passed a weary hand across her eyes. Was it really only eighteen months ago that she had accompanied her father to her first really adult party since leaving school —the annual presentation of awards within the United Publishing Group in the penthouse suite of their towering City building? The girl who had arrived at the party on Sir Charles Trevor's arm, in a secret flutter of excitement, seemed to have come from a different world. Not long past eighteen, with three good 'A' levels under her belt, and the world her oyster, it had seemed. Or, at least, the world as delineated by her father. It had disappointed her to discover that her dreams of university were to remain dreams for the time being. Sir Charles, it seemed, needed her to act as his hostess, and he had informed her that it would do her no harm to learn how to run the London house, and Branthwaite, his home in Berkshire. Briony had been frankly unenthusiastic at the prospect. For one thing, she could imagine the reaction from Mrs Lambert, their briskly efficient housekeeper, if she attempted to interfere in the clockwork running of either establishment. For another, she had always planned on having a career of some sort, and she told her father so.

Sir Charles had raised his eyebrows. 'I've no objection to you finding yourself a job of sorts in time, Briony,' he said. 'But I do hope you're not intending to turn yourself into one of these strident females, always demanding equal opportunities, and other nonsense. Besides, I did think you might wish to give me some of your time now that your full-time education has been completed. I've been very lonely since your mother died, and I was looking forward to your companionship.'

Which was emotional blackmail at the very least, Briony thought gloomily as she murmured reluctant acquiescence. She was neither blind nor stupid, and she was quite aware that her father had consoled himself during the latter years of his widowhood with a succession of attractive ladies, many of whom had been only too willing to act as his hostess. She wondered rather acidly whether the subtle pressures on her father to remarry had proved rather overwhelming of late, and if that was why she was being dragged kicking and screaming into the picture.

But she consoled herself with the thought that the next year or so could be fun. There would be dinners and receptions, and even trips abroad, and a greater contrast to the boarding school life of past years could scarcely be envisaged. Her father had been too busy controlling the publishing empire of which he was chairman to have paid her a great deal of attention up to now.

The dinner which had preceded the awards party had been rather a disappointment to her. She had been introduced to a number of young executives, who had paid her flattering attention, but she was realistic to know that this was what she could expect as the chairman's daughter, even if she'd had two heads. She was not unaware of her own attractions—her slender figure, the sheen of her coppery hair, and the charm of her wide-set grey-green eyes with their heavy fringing of lashes—and was becoming used to the glances which tended to follow her these days. But at the same time she knew there had to be a happy medium between the overt flattery of the younger men at U.P.G. and the almost paternal deference of the older ones. She guessed that her father's reputation of being a hard man to cross was responsible for the respectful distance which seemed to be maintained from them for most of the evening.

When the actual moment for the awards came, Briony quite enjoyed handing over the small silver replicas of quill pens, and the accompanying cheques, and uttering a few shy words of congratulation to writers, photographers and artists who had been merely names to her up to now.

She was just beginning to shed some of her inhibitions and enjoy being the centre of the stage, when she became aware of a man watching her across the room. For a moment their eyes met and locked, and Briony was teased by an odd sense of familiarity. But she knew he was not one of those she had met at the dinner.

And in the same moment she realised that the expression in the aquamarine-pale eyes, looking her over from head to foot, was neither paternal nor deferential. It was coolly challenging, even faintly amused, and it told Briony quite clearly and unequivocally that wherever the sex war was waged, this man would expect to emerge as a victor. Nor did she have to wonder how anyone of her age and inexperience, only recently released from the shelter of school, could have known this. It was pure instinct, and she recognised it as such.

But all the same, she turned away hurriedly, aware that embarrassment mingled with indignation was heightening the colour in her face, and was annoyed to find that her mind still retained an image of him, tall and lean, his tawny hair bleached into blond streaks, and his eyes startlingly pale against the deep tan of his face.

All she had to do, of course, was wait until her father, deep in conversation with Hal Mackenzie, the editor of the *Courier*, the group's leading and influential daily paper, was free, and then ask the man's name. But she was reluctant to do this, for reasons she only dimly perceived herself. Something told her that if her father wished her to know this man, then he would have arranged for there to be an introduction earlier in the evening.

In the event, she did not have to wait to be told who he was. When the time came for the prestigious 'Journalist of the Year' award to be made, and the name Logan Adair was called, he walked forward. As she picked up the award, Briony discovered crossly that the palms of her hands were damp, but she managed to present a calm exterior as Logan Adair shook hands, first with her father, who was murmuring a few conventional phrases of congratulation, and then turned to her.

She said politely, 'Well done, Mr Adair,' in a small, cool voice, and held out his award and envelope. Everyone else had taken their award, thanked her, shaken hands and walked away, usually back to the bar with ill-concealed relief. But not Logan Adair.

He said with elaborate courtesy, 'On the contrary, thank you, my dear Miss Trevor,' and his hand reached out to clasp not her fingers as she expected, but her wrist, pulling her forward towards him slightly off balance, so that she looked up in quick alarm and saw the amused glint in his eyes before he deliberately lowered his mouth to hers. The pressure was quick and light, and casual in the extreme, so there was no reason on earth why Briony should jerk back as if she had been branded, only to find the little incident had been witnessed in the loudest silence she had ever heard.

Logan Adair said smilingly, 'A pleasure to have met you, Miss Trevor,' and turned away.

Briony's cheeks were stained with bright colour and her fragile poise was shaken to its core. The chatter round the room had broken out again, but too loudly, and out of the corner of her eye she saw Sir Charles, frowning thunderously, wheel on Hal Mackenzie. She wished with all her heart, in spite of her embarrassment, that her father would treat it as the joke it had undoubtedly been, or else forget it altogether, but she knew this could never happen.

Sir Charles was well known for his ambivalent attitude to the empire he controlled, she thought unhappily. He was proud of his newspapers and magazines and the influence they wielded, yet he had little time for the rank and file journalists and photographers who provided the words and pictures for his millions of readers to pore over. United Publishing had had its fair share of industrial troubles in the past, and Briony was aware that many people in the organisation believed that their chairman's intransigent attitude towards his workforce was at least partly to blame.

'What Charles would really like to see would be complete automation in the industry, complete with robots to press the right buttons,' an old friend had remarked recently at a private dinner party, and though Briony had joined in the laughter which followed, the comment had troubled her slightly. It occurred to her that a newspaper's quality was largely dictated by the people who wrote for it. People like Logan Adair, whose byline appeared above hard-hitting eye-witness reports from the trouble spots of the globe.

Briony had seen his name often in the *Courier*, and had looked out for his stories, relishing his laconic style and the dry humour with which he often laced the bitter truth he had to tell. She knew from comments she had heard that he was regarded as one of the feathers in the *Courier*'s cap, and that there were plenty of rival newspapers who would have paid over the odds to obtain his services, but she was also aware that her father did not share these sentiments.

She heard Hal Mackenzie say placatingly, 'Sir Charles, isn't this all rather a storm in a tea-cup?' and walked away hastily. The presentations were over, fortunately, and someone had opened the french doors at the end of the room which led out on to the rooftop terrace. She was glad to be able to escape there, and glad too to find herself alone. If indeed she was alone. She'd only taken one long steadying breath of the crisp night air when she was aware that she was being watched, and turned quickly. When she saw just who it was standing between her and the door, she stepped back involuntarily, her heart missing a beat.

Logan Adair said acidly, 'There's no need to panic, Miss Trevor. Our brief encounter just now didn't drive me so mad with desire that I've rushed out here to ravish you.'

'Then why precisely did you—rush out here, Mr Adair? To insult me again?'

The pale eyes held a wry gleam as he looked at her. He said, 'My God, that has the authentic Trevor stamp on it! As a matter of fact, I think I had some vague idea of making amends, but I'm sure your father's daughter would regard that as a sign of weakness, so I think I'll return to the more congenial atmosphere at the bar.'

He was already turning away as she said, 'I'm sorry if I overreacted. You—startled me, that's all.'

'And not for the first time this evening.' He shook his head slightly. 'I always understood that sweet sixteen was the limit for never having been kissed. You're two years out of date.'

'How do you know how old I am?' she demanded.

'Elementary, my sweet. The *Courier* too has its gossip column, and your eighteenth birthday was featured with photographs—remember? "The lovely Briony Trevor comes of age" it said, rather predictably. Claridges, wasn't it? My invitation must have been mislaid somewhere.'

She tried to match his own light tone. 'You mean you would have accepted one?'

'Probably not,' he said drily. 'But I think I'd make a point of being around the day you really come of age.'

There was a sudden stillness between them, a tension that was almost tangible. He hadn't really retreated at all, Briony realised. He was still firmly entrenched between her and the door that led back to the party and safety. She felt herself becoming flustered and knew it was important to conceal the fact.

She said rather hurriedly, 'Why did you do it? Kiss me, I mean?'

'Call it an irresistible urge.'

'Do you often have them?'

'Not as often as I seem to be having them this evening,' he said mockingly, and grinned at her. 'I must admit the original urge was more to test the depth of that immaculate boarding school poise rather than to arouse wanton desires in your undoubtedly virginal breast. I also wanted to annoy your father.'

'Well, you've succeeded in that,' she said coldly, oddly disappointed that he apparently had seen her as a schoolgirl to be teased.

'So I noticed. I think poor old Mac is being ordered to carpet me first thing on Monday morning—or fire me at the earliest opportunity. Probably both. And if your father realised I was alone with you now, he wouldn't even wait for Monday morning.'

'I think you're exaggerating,' she said. 'You don't fire the Journalist of the Year simply because he annoys you at a party.'

'You might do,' he said. 'If you were Sir Charles Trevor, and if the journalist in question had been a thorn in your flesh for some considerable time.' His lips curled slightly. 'And as it looks as if I'm going to be hanged anyway, it may as well be for a sheep as a lamb . . .'

He took an unhurried step forward and his arms reached for her, drawing her effortlessly against him. 'You should have been kissed before, Briony,' he said huskily, and then his mouth came down on hers.

His lips were warm and seeking and very enticing. Her arms slid up around his neck, almost of their own volition, holding him closer still as the kiss deepened from the gently exploratory to the frankly demanding. In the end, it was Logan who pulled away, his breathing a little ragged, his eyes narrowing speculatively as he looked down at her.

'I don't know what you have in mind for the remainder of the evening,' he said with a touch of grimness. 'But I sure as hell know it won't be what I'm thinking of right now, so I think you'd better return to the safety of your father's side, Miss Trevor. Believe me, it will be better for both of us.'

'Scared, Mr Adair?' Briony's heart was pounding suffocatingly as she looked up at him through her lashes. She was being deliberately provocative and she knew it, enjoying the first heady taste of a woman's power over the man who finds her desirable.

'Hardly, Miss Trevor,' he drawled. 'But I guarantee you would be, if I decided to continue this romantic moment to its obvious conclusion. Don't play with fire, darling, because it's a very good way of ending up scorched, and I imagine Daddy would prefer to hand you over to the bridegroom of his choice not even slightly singed.'

She felt destroyed by his cynicism. She said angrily, 'You're not irresistible, you know. And I'll choose my own husband!'

'Brave words.' He smiled faintly. 'But you'll need more than that to stand up against your father. Believe me, I know.'

She was just going to ask him how he knew—to demand the information if necessary, when a woman's voice said impatiently, 'Logan, so this is where you've got to!'

Briony recognised her instantly. It was Karen Wellesley, the *Courier*'s women's editor, a slim shapely blonde in her late twenties, with one broken marriage already behind her. Karen moved forward to Logan's side, sliding an openly possessive hand through his arm.

'Good God,' she remarked rather blankly as her exotically made-up eyes fell on Briony. 'I do hope I'm not interrupting anything.'

'Nothing at all,' Logan assured her coolly. 'Miss Trevor and I were just having an interesting discussion on the nature of choice, but we'd reached stalemate.'

'That's all right, then.' Karen smiled blindingly up at him. 'The party's beginning to break up, and I thought you might like to take me somewhere to celebrate your award.'

He said lightly, 'I'd be more than delighted, my love, if Miss Trevor will excuse us.'

Briony said, 'Of course.' She gave them both a taut little smile. 'If the party's breaking up, then my father will be ready to leave.'

She walked past them, her chin in the air, and made for the lighted doorway. She was thankful to see her father absorbed in conversation with some of the members of the Board, his bad humour apparently forgotten for the moment.

'Hello, sweetheart.' His glance smilingly embraced her as she joined him. 'Where have you been?'

'I—I went out to get some air,' she said. 'I think I have a headache starting. Do you think we could leave soon?'

He was all concern, immediately getting someone to ring down and have his car brought round to the main entrance of the building, fussing protectively as one of the maids hired for the evening went to fetch Briony's wrap. They were standing waiting for the lift to come up, surrounded by a small group of her father's colleagues from the upper echelons of management, when Logan came out of the penthouse suite into the corridor, with Karen moulded so closely to his side that a casual spectator might have assumed she was welded there. And Briony discovered to her acute vexation that she was far from being a casual observer.

She transferred her attention almost painfully to the row of lights which indicated the floor that the lift had reached, and saw with relief that it was almost at the top.

She heard Logan say, 'Come on, love. We'll walk down two floors. There's something I want to fetch from my desk.'

She felt them move away. She wouldn't let herself turn and look, because she knew it would cause her pain.

As the lift descended Sir Charles said abruptly, 'You behaved very well this evening, Briony. I was pleased with you.' His brow darkened. 'I'm sorry that Adair fellow couldn't behave himself.'

Briony said with difficulty, 'It—it really doesn't matter, Daddy. It wasn't important.'

Her father snorted, but made no further comment, to her relief. In the car the inevitable briefcase was produced, and he became immersed in his papers while Briony sat quietly, a prey to her thoughts.

There had been a lot of first times that evening, she told herself. Her first really adult party, her first kiss, and now the realisation that one's first awakening to the demands that passion might impose was not necessarily a happy one, because where passion went, jealousy and loneliness trod on his heels.

And lying in bed that night, Briony thought of Logan and Karen together, and was both jealous and lonely.

Briony roused herself with a start, becoming aware of her surroundings again, dragging herself back half-unwillingly to the present.

Jealousy, loneliness and pain, she thought unhappily,

as she knelt to tend the fire which had burned low during her reverie. Those ugly words seemed to encompass the whole miserable history of her brief marriage. Why hadn't she realised that first night what would happen, and held aloof? But she knew the answer to that—because she was already in the thrall of an attraction which she was not experienced enough to resist. And besides the undoubted glamour of Logan Adair's personality, there had also been the beguiling prospect of living dangerously, of rebelling against her father's plans and prejudices. It was a situation fraught with pitfalls, but quite irresistible to the child she had been.

If her marriage to Logan had taught her nothing else, she thought detachedly, it had taught her to put away childish things.

But, if this was true, why had she run away? That was the act of a child, not the woman she believed she had become.

It had been the shattering shock of Logan's return which had forced her into flight, she thought. For months she had lived with the knowledge that he was dead—executed in the Middle Eastern oil state of Azabia where he had been covering a revolutionary coup by the new government. 'A spy for the Western powers', the brief communiqué had stated. No further details had been given, and his body had not been returned. The Embassy could do nothing because they were themselves enduring a state of siege for some weeks following the coup, and were later evacuated.

But the report of Logan's death had seemed more like an epilogue than the finale to the tragic farce that had been their marriage. The news had shattered her, yet their relationship had finished long before Logan ever left for Azabia. Over, she thought, her lips twisting painfully, almost before it had begun, in disillusionment on her side and contempt on his.

But even if things had been different, could such an ill-matched marriage ever have stood a chance? she wondered sadly.

Even on the first evening they had met, she had been aware of the gulf which yawned between them. Logan at thirty-four was a man of the world, cynical, knowledgeable and experienced. She had been a naïve schoolgirl, looking for a hero to worship. Only Logan had no wish to be cast in the heroic mould. He'd made that clear from the beginning, but she wouldn't listen. She'd been deaf to every hint, every warning except the clamouring of her own instincts, and they had played her false.

She had found it difficult to sleep that night after the party—the first of many sleepless nights. And she was being a fool, she told herself, as she viewed the shadows that sleeplessness had left under her eyes. So she had been kissed. So what? A lot of girls her age were already married, and mothers, not necessarily in that order. Just because she had spent the last few years at a school where even the most casual relationships with the opposite sex were frowned on it didn't mean she had to make a big emotional deal out of one kiss.

She found herself wondering if she would have been doing all this heart-searching if she had been kissed by one of the young executives who had been discreetly clustering round prior to the awards presentation.

She sighed as she picked up a brush and began rather listlessly to stroke it down the length of her dark copper hair. The only way she could find out, it seemed, would be to allow herself to be taken out by one of U.P.G.'s bright young men and kissed so that she could compare notes. It was not a prospect that held any appeal for her at all.

What she really wanted, she thought quite calmly, was for Logan to kiss her again. She leaned forward, peering at herself intently in the dressing-table mirror, touching her fingers to the softness of her lips, and wondering why a girl's mouth should be so vulnerable when a man's was hard and bruising. She began to wish she had emulated many of her contemporaries at school, and had secret romances concealed at peril of expulsion from the staff. At least now, she would not feel so totally confused and at a loss. She knew all about her body's biological processes, but very little about its emotional needs, which, she had begun to suspect, were far more complex.

She was quiet at breakfast, causing her father to enquire anxiously whether her headache was still persisting.

'No, I'm fine,' she assured him, pushing aside her boiled egg, untasted. 'Daddy, I've been thinking. It's time I started work—got myself a job.'

Sir Charles touched his table napkin to his lips and laid it to one side.

He said with a hint of impatience, 'My dear Briony, I thought we agreed that you should spend this year at least working for me—learning how to run this house, and how to act as my hostess.'

'That's hardly a fulltime occupation,' she protested. 'And I have to find something to do.' She picked up the silver pot and added more coffee to her cup. She said too casually, 'My English marks were always good. I was wondering if I couldn't become a journalist.'

She stole a swift glance at her father and saw his brows had drawn together in a thunderous frown.

'You can't be serious,' he said at last.

'Why not?'

'If you need to be enlightened on the point, then I will do so. A newspaper office is no place for any woman, and particularly not for my daughter.'

'But lots of women work on newspapers,' she said. 'Many of them work on your newspapers.'

'Not at my wish,' he said coldly. 'But in these days of sex equality, it's impossible to exercise any proper discrimination.'

'Oh, Daddy!' Briony suddenly didn't know whether to laugh or cry. 'You really are appallingly prejudiced!'

'Am I? Perhaps so, but I stand by every word I've said. Newspaper reporters are hard—the nature of the job they do makes them so, and whereas a degree of toughness and cynicism is acceptable and excusable in a man, it cannot be so in a girl.' He folded his newspaper and rose to his feet. 'I would not wish to see you losing your essential sensitivity, my dear, becoming coarse and uncaring in your attitude. I...'

'Daddy,' Briony cut in impatiently, 'I can't believe what I'm hearing! You've been in the newspaper business all your life, yet you give the impression that you hate it.'

'Sometimes I do,' her father said quietly. 'Particularly I hate what it does to people. I'd hate what it might do to you.' He glanced at his watch. 'I must be going now. I have a full day ahead of me.'

And I have an empty one, she thought soberly, as the door closed behind him. She had not been altogether serious in her suggestion that she should become a journalist. It had been more of a passing thought, than a burning ambition, but the idea seemed to gain in attraction as she considered it. Besides, it was time she began to think for herself and plan her life. Many girls whose examination results had not nearly been as good as hers were starting at university, and in some ways she wished she had insisted on going too, but Sir Charles had been so emphatic that he wanted her at home, that it had seemed ungracious to persist. And at that time, the prospect of several more years in academic pursuits had not seemed very alluring.

But her father surely couldn't expect her to spend all her time sitting round the house twiddling her thumbs. He knew perfectly well that all the real work was done by Mrs Lambert, with the assistance of a daily help, and that Briony's place in the scheme of things was a supernumary one. Or did he think she was going to get married almost at once?

Unwillingly she found herself recalling what Logan Adair had said about her choice of a husband, and a sudden image rose in her mind of herself, white-gowned and bridal-veiled, walking up an aisle of a church to where a faceless man awaited her by the altar, waited for her to be handed over to him by her father—untouched by human hand or by life itself.

She felt an hysterical giggle rising in her throat at the thought. Could it be possible to allow oneself to be bored into matrimony—to exchange the dullness of one safe existence for another without even being tempted to taste the danger and adventure of real life?

She pushed her chair back abruptly and stood up. University would have been her first encounter with an unsheltered world, and she had been baulked of that. She could not afford to let another opportunity pass her by.

She would go round to the U.P.G. building and ask Hal Mackenzie of the *Courier* for a job. He had been very pleasant when she had met him the previous evening, she tried to bolster her confidence, and she had all the requisite qualifications on paper.

Besides, she thought not too hopefully, if she was successful in obtaining a job, however junior, on the most serious and influential paper in the group, perhaps her father would become resigned or even sympathetic to her aspirations. At least she would make him see she was not merely a cipher with no mind of her own. She had nothing to lose by trying.

But she was already on her way to the U.P.G. offices when the disturbing thought struck her that she might have a great deal to lose. That by deliberately seeking to place herself in close proximity to Logan Adair, she could well end up by losing her heart.

'And I did,' Briony thought in anguish, staring sightlessly into the fire. 'Oh, God, I did!'

And her tears, slow and heavy, tasted salt upon her trembling mouth.

CHAPTER TWO

SHE cried for some time, sitting hunched in her high-backed chair, her hands pressed to her face. She was crying primarily, she knew, because she was tired and emotionally confused, but some of her tears were for the hopeful, vulnerable child who had thought all she needed to do was stretch out her hand for what she wanted.

She could even smile at the innocent arrogance which had taken her straight to the editor of one of Fleet Street's leading dailies to ask for a job.

Looking back, she had to admit that Hal Mackenzie had let her down lightly. He had listened quite seriously to her stumbling exposition of why she thought a career in journalism would suit her, and had even made a few notes on the pad in front of him as she talked. He had asked courteously what her shorthand speed was, and had made no comment when she confessed she had never done any. He had lifted a number of closely printed sheets from his in-tray and handed them to her, asking her to go into his secretary's office next door and produce a news-story from the handout, no more than six paragraphs long. Briony's heart sank as she sat before the gleaming electric typewriter and read the mass of words and statistics the handout contained. She was miserably conscious as she handed her finished story to Hal Mackenzie that it would fall far short of the standard required, and saw his brows rise slightly as he read it through.

He put it down on his desk, removed the heavy horn-rimmed glasses he wore and wiped them carefully on a spotless white handkerchief while an unnerving silence lengthened.

He said at last, 'Miss Trevor, I've a friend in the Midlands who runs a small group of weekly papers. It's a good training ground, and if I recommended you to him he would give you a chance.'

Briony said, 'But I thought ...' and paused.

Hal Mackenzie said drily, 'You hoped your relationship with the Chairman would open doors for you at U.P.G. Well, I'm afraid not, even if you'd been incredibly talented, which you're not. But you could probably learn to be reasonably competent in time, with a sound provincial training behind you. Well, shall I write to my friend on your behalf?' He waited, watching as the embarrassed flush deepened in her cheeks, then sighed. 'Miss Trevor, I'm old enough to be your father, so may I give you some sound advice? Don't read too much into a few moonlight kisses.'

Briony said lamely, 'I don't know what you mean.'

'No?' His brows rose. 'I saw Logan follow you, you know. Fortunately your father didn't. He'd already made his views on what had happened earlier quite clear.'

'Mr Mackenzie,' Briony made a belated grab for the remnants of her poise, 'it really isn't what you think ...'

'Isn't it?' His tone was sceptical. 'You're a very lovely girl, Miss Trevor. Believe me, I'm not trying to censure either Logan or yourself. Good God, if I was twenty years younger, I'd probably have tried to beat him to it, no matter who or what your father was. Does he know you've come here to ask for a job, incidentally?'

Briony bit her lip. 'We've—discussed it, naturally ...'

'In other words, no.' Mackenzie sighed again. 'It won't do, Miss Trevor. I can't imagine Sir Charles tamely accepting a life in journalism for you. I shall speak frankly to you. He's a good chairman, but his heart is not in newspapers, the way your grandfather's was. I often think your father would have been just as happy—happier even—making cars, or sewing machines. Something that couldn't talk back. Sometimes he acts as if journalism was a dirty word.' He gave her a wry look. 'And even if he didn't, I wouldn't consider passing over some of the good people who apply to me for work in order to give a start to an untrained girl with no particular flair. As it is, I'm afraid your father's known views would have to weigh with me—plus my own misgivings about your possible motivation.'

'I hardly think that's any of your business.' She felt hot with humiliation.

'That's where you're wrong.' He gave her a shrewd look. 'I like my newspaper to operate efficiently, with my staff giving me their best efforts. That's why I don't encourage—personal situations, shall we say? They tend to get in the way in office hours. Sometimes, of course, relationships become established, and I have to accept them. All my staff are adults, after all.'

Briony said coolly, 'If you're trying to bestow a paternal warning that Logan Adair has a—relationship with

Miss Wellesley, then please don't bother. I already know. I'm sorry to have taken up so much of your time. And there's no need to write to your friend. I'm sure they need someone with flair—even in the provinces.'

He rose, as she did. 'You make me sound an insensitive brute, Miss Trevor, and I'm sorry. But it wouldn't work, believe me—oh, for all sorts of reasons. It may seem a glamorous life from the outside, but it's hard work and pain with very little room for idealism, whatever pious platitudes we editors may utter from time to time. I think you're still young enough to have ideals, so why not find yourself a star to hitch your wagon to? And please forgive me for having spoken so frankly on matters which were—not my concern.'

There were tears stinging Briony's eyes as she hurried across the outer office and out into the corridor, ignoring the embarrassed secretary. She paused for a moment to snatch a pair of dark glasses from her handbag and cram them on to her nose to hide the most visible signs of her discomfiture. There were people waiting at the lift, so she took the stairs down to the ground floor. There was a women's cloakroom there, and she slipped inside for a few moments, to effect a few repairs to her make-up. When she was sure she was in complete control once more, she walked out into the reception area and towards the massive glass doors which guarded the main entrance to the building.

And Logan Adair crossed the reception area just in front of her and went out into the street, pausing to hold open the doors for a group of women who were entering.

Briony stood stock still for a minute, hardly able to believe her eyes. To see him so suddenly, and unexpectedly, seemed like a sign, a good omen. If she'd taken the lift, if she hadn't waited to fix her make-up, then she would have missed him. She hurried to the door and out on to the pavement. He was just ahead of her waiting to cross the road, flicking the folded newspaper he carried against his leg in slight impatience as he watched the stream of traffic. There was no reason in the world why she shouldn't approach him, say something light and laughing about coincidences, and it being a small world, but she couldn't do it, so she held back slightly, and then followed him as he crossed the road. She'd no idea, of course, where he was going. He might even be working on a story, but she didn't think so. After all, he was in the foreign news department, not the City desk. Far more likely, she thought, glancing at her watch, that he was taking an early lunch. He did not seem to be in any particular hurry, strolling along in the pale sunshine, and Briony had little difficulty in keeping him in sight. Meanwhile a couple of disquieting thoughts occurred to her. What would she do if he turned and saw her skulking after him, and—which was infinitely worse—what if he was going to keep some lunchtime appointment with Karen Wellesley?

Her heart sank, but her spirits revived miraculously a moment later when Logan turned quite casually into the entrance of a large street-corner pub. After only a moment's hesitation she followed him. After the brightness of the street, the interior seemed dim. Although it was still relatively early, many of the tables and velvet-covered benches along the walls were already occupied, and an appetisingly savoury smell hung in the air. Briony took a deep breath, then walked up to the bar.

Logan was just turning away, drink in hand, as she reached it. He saw her at once, and recognised her immediately in spite of the dark glasses, and his brows rose with amazed incredulity.

'Slumming, Miss Trevor?'

'It hardly looks like a slum to me, Mr Adair.' Her

voice sounded cool and composed, and she even managed a smile to match.

'But hardly your usual stamping ground, I would have thought.' He smiled too, but the cool eyes held a puzzled, almost reflective expression as he studied her. 'Will you let me buy you a drink?'

'Thank you.' She hastily suppressed a feeling of glee. 'You—you're not expecting anyone?'

'No one,' he said, a touch drily. 'The house wine is good here, and so is the food—unless you're going on somewhere for lunch.' His eyes wandered over the simple chic of the cream wool suit, and the dark green blouse she wore beneath it, all designed to convince Hal Mackenzie of her mature efficiency.

'I'd heard the food was marvellous,' she fibbed hastily. 'That's why I thought I'd try it.'

'How word does get around!' He did not bother to disguise his scepticism. 'But it isn't patronised much at Board room level. They have their own dining room, I believe.' He handed her a menu. 'I can recommend the shepherd's pie.'

'That will be fine.' She would have sampled boiled wellington boots on his recommendation, she thought dazedly. Logan gave the order to the barmaid, then ushered her to a couple of vacant seats on one of the benches under a long window. The sun poured through the glass, and she was glad to unbutton her jacket and slip it from her shoulders, arching her body slightly. As she did so, Logan's eyes flickered momentarily over the rounded outline of her breasts, revealed through the fragile silky texture of her blouse.

'Allow me.' He helped her with the jacket, and for a second his hand rested on her shoulder and she felt its warmth on her flesh as if she had been naked. She stole a glance at him under her lashes, and saw that his face looked rather grim as he put her glass of white wine in front of her. She had to stifle the feeling of excited triumph that was beginning to build up inside her. The sophisticated Mr Adair was as aware of her, as she was of him, she told herself in delirious unbelief. Almost imperceptibly she edged nearer to him on the bench.

'Do you smoke?' He produced a packet of Gauloises and a lighter from the pocket of his brown cord jacket and held them out to her. She shook her head silently.

'Good girl.' He sounded lazily amused. 'All the virtues and none of the vices, which is just as it should be at eighteen. Do you object if I smoke?'

'Not at all.' Suddenly tongue-tied, she picked up her wine-glass and sipped, enjoying the cool fragrance of the wine in her dry mouth. She searched around nervously for something to say. 'Did—did you enjoy the awards party.'

'Parts of it—very much.' The amusement was open now, and she felt herself blush. 'But the awards themselves are pretty meaningless.'

'Why do you say that?'

'I don't need an ornament for my mantelpiece,' he said. 'I'm rarely at the flat long enough at a stretch to appreciate the fact that I have a mantelpiece anyway. And while the money is welcome, it's not exactly essential. U.P.G. are quite generous in the matter of salaries, whatever your father's personal feelings about his staff. I suspect that many awards presentations do more for the self-esteem of the donors than the recipients.'

'But doesn't it mean anything to you to be Journalist of the Year?' she persisted.

He shrugged slightly. 'Most of these titles are meaningless,' he said. 'It pleases me far more to know that Mac appreciates me and likes my work. He's a good bloke to work for.'

'Unfortunately I'll never be in a position to judge the truth of that statement.' Briony stared down at the polished surface of their table.

'Meaning?'

'Meaning I asked Mr Mackenzie for a job, and he turned me down flat—not half an hour ago, as a matter of fact.'

'You wanted to work on the *Courier*?' Logan set down his glass so sharply that some of the liquid splashed out of it.

'Is it so surprising?' she enquired defensively.

'Amazing would be a better word.' He gave her a long speculative look. 'Now what could have put such an unlikely idea into your decorative head, Miss Trevor?'

'Kindly don't patronise me,' she said unevenly. 'And don't reduce me to the level of another mantelpiece ornament either.'

'Is that what I was doing?' He smiled drily. 'I can assure you it's a very different item of furniture which suggests itself when I look at you.'

'Oh!' A faint flush rose in her cheeks as she absorbed the implication of what he had said, and she hated herself for blushing like a fool at his teasing. She said hastily, 'Nevertheless I did apply for a job on the *Courier*, but Mr Mackenzie unfortunately seemed to share your incredulity.'

Logan said coolly, 'He also possesses a well-developed sense of self-preservation—an excellent asset for anyone hoping to make progress on one of your father's newspapers. Apart from your youth, and your total inexperience, I imagine that went a long way towards your rejection by him.'

'I really don't see what my father has to do with it,' Briony said, nettled.

'Oh, come on, love.' His eyebrows rose. 'You're surely

not trying to make me believe you're that naïve? Your father tends to shed his newspaper personnel like autumn leaves, and you know it, or you should do. Besides, if Mac had given you a job, he'd probably have had trouble with the union to face, as well as your father. The *Courier* isn't a training school for beginners.'

She said in a stifled tone, 'Well, he didn't give me a job, so there's very little point in discussing it.'

'Yet it still rankles.' He shot her a look. 'Was it this job that was so important to you, or any job?'

'I wanted to work—to be of some use.' She shrugged. 'I thought journalism would suit me, that's all.'

He gave her an amused glance. 'And to start at the top would suit you even better? Nice try, sweetheart. But if you really wanted a job, why didn't you apply to Vic Hargreaves in Personnel? There are usually vacancies of sorts somewhere in the group.'

'I didn't think of it,' she admitted. 'You see, I'd met Mr Mackenzie, and he seemed kind, so I thought I'd take a chance . . .' Her voice tailed off a little as she saw he was laughing quite openly now. 'What have I said?'

'Your reference to Mac's apparent kindness. I doubt if it's the image he has of himself. Anyway, here comes the food. I hope you're hungry.'

At that particular moment, Briony felt as if she could not have forced a morsel past the tightness in her throat, but it was odd when the steaming plate was placed in front of her, how her appetite suddenly returned. The shepherd's pie was deliciously savoury, flanked by lavish spoonfuls of carrots and peas, and she finished every forkful with real appreciation.

'Would you like something to follow?' asked Logan.

'I couldn't eat another thing.' She leaned back with a little sigh of satisfaction. 'Some coffee, maybe, that's all. I don't want to get fat.'

'I don't think there's much danger of that.' His cool gaze wandered over her, lingering deliberately on her slender waist and the flatness of her stomach. 'A few pounds wouldn't hurt you.'

She laughed, finishing off the wine left in her glass. 'This must be my day for being put down! I hoped you'd say I was perfect as I was.'

'But perfection doesn't appeal to me,' he said. 'A few failings add humanity.' He signalled to the waitress and ordered the coffee, while Briony sat beside him in silence, her thoughts whirling. Once the coffee was drunk, then this all too brief lunch would be over, and how was she ever going to see him again? She couldn't hang about outside the U.P.G. offices every day on the offchance of meeting him. And this meal hadn't gone quite as she'd hoped. Last night he had made no secret of her attraction for him. Today he had teased her a little, but his manner had generally been wary, even a little aloof at times. There had been moments when his mouth had looked almost grim, and it was difficult to remember how it had felt when it had touched hers. All that she knew was that she longed for him to remind her what it had been like.

She moistened her lips with the tip of her tongue. 'Where did you work before you joined the *Courier*?'

'I was on a provincial daily in the North, doing mostly investigative work. But I'd always wanted to work abroad and when I heard there was a vacancy on the *Courier*'s foreign news department, I applied for it.' He lifted an eyebrow. 'Does that satisfy your curiosity, or do you want the story of my life? It isn't very interesting.'

'Well, it can't possibly be as dull as mine,' she said rather ruefully. 'And of course it interests me. I'd hardly . . .' She paused.

'You'd hardly be here with me now, if you weren't—interested,' he finished for her.

She hunched a shoulder. 'If you don't want to tell me——' she began, but he cut across her impatiently.

'It isn't that, Briony. I'll tell you anything you want to know, but I must admit you puzzle me.'

'Do I?' She sent him a dazzling smile. 'Well, that's a good start.'

'I wasn't aware that we were starting anything!' He paused to pay the waitress as she brought their coffee and the bill. When she had gone, he said quietly, 'Now let's have the truth. Just why are you here—and please don't feed me any more nonsense about having heard rave reports of the food.'

She said blandly, 'I saw you coming in here, and I didn't want to have lunch alone. Satisfied?'

'Not entirely. I could name at random at least half a dozen young executives that you met last night who would give a large proportion of their handsome salaries to take you somewhere fashionable to eat for a couple of hours. Why me?'

She shrugged. 'Perhaps none of them forced themselves on my attention in quite the same way, Mr Adair.'

'So you decided to employ the same tactics?' That reflective, considering look was back.

'Why not? Last night I got the impression you found me attractive. If I'm wrong, you can always claim this lunch back off your expenses.'

'Attractive isn't quite the appropriate word,' he said slowly. 'I find you both desirable and exasperating—not always in equal or even the same proportions.'

'How very odd,' Briony said sweetly. 'I find you exectly the same. But you were going to tell me about your early life.'

'Yes, I was, wasn't I?' he said pleasantly. 'It's perfectly

simple. I'm thirty-four, unmarried, and my parents are both dead. I was educated at a grammar school, and from there I went on to Oxford where I read politics, philosophy and economics. I came into journalism as a graduate entrant, which isn't a bad way to start. In my time, I've covered every type of story from funerals and flower shows to murder hunts and corruption. Is that what you wanted to know?'

'You know it wasn't,' she said in a low voice, and for a moment there was silence between them. When she looked up at him again, she was smiling, and her eyes under the deep sweep of lashes were deliberately provocative. 'Your past wasn't very productive,' she murmured. 'Perhaps I'll have better luck with your future.' She reached out and took his hand, turning it palm upwards for her inspection. 'Hmm.' She bent over it, pretending absorption, one pink-tipped finger tracing the various lines on his hand as she spoke. 'A strong headline, but then I'd expect that. A long lifeline, and quite steady too, except for your middle years which could hold some danger for you ...'

'Never more than at this moment, I suspect.' His tone was dry. 'Briony, what are you trying to do.'

'Tell your fortune,' she said with mock innocence. 'Now your heartline is really fascinating. I would say you could get any woman you wanted, merely by asking.'

'Now that is fascinating,' he said gravely. 'Your coffee's getting cold.'

'You don't think I know what I'm talking about,' she accused.

'I think I know exactly what you're talking about,' he said. 'And it has nothing to do with palmistry. Tell me something, Briony. When we leave here, what are your plans for the rest of the afternoon?'

Her heart suddenly seemed to miss a beat at the question. 'I—I don't have anything planned.'

'No?' His hand closed round hers, opening it palm upwards. 'Now it's my turn, and I'll tell you what I see. I see the heartline dominating the head. I see a mixed-up girl who doesn't know what she wants. I see a dangerous craving for excitement in the lifeline, but this evens out before too long into steadiness and security and a suitable marriage.'

Briony snatched her hand away. 'But that isn't what I want,' she said unevenly. 'And you know it. What—what are your plans for the rest of the afternoon?' She died all kinds of small deaths while she waited for him to answer.

'I think they could best be described as fluid,' Logan said slowly at last. 'But they certainly begin with more coffee—at my flat, I think. Shall we go and find a taxi?'

She had thought that he would kiss her in the taxi, but he didn't, and she felt dashed by this. He hardly spoke either, and his face was suddenly remote as if his thoughts had travelled a long way from her, and she did not dare make any attempt to recall them. But by the time the taxi drew up in front of the small block of flats where Logan lived, she was feeling thoroughly nervous and on edge.

He didn't put his arm around her either as they went up the stairs to the first floor, and she felt oddly chilled as he fitted the key into the lock and admitted her to a small cramped hall. There were a couple of letters lying just inside the door and he bent to retrieve them, slitting them open carelessly with his thumbnail and running his eye over the contents while she stood, waiting. He was being so casual, she thought, as though this happened all the time, as maybe it did with him, but not with her as he surely must realise.

She wasn't just nervous any more either. She was definitely panicky, and suddenly and paralysingly shy at the thought of what she was doing. She had never dreamed she could behave in this way, but she'd thought that Logan would somehow make it easy for her. After all, it was last night's kisses which had set off the chain reaction which had brought her to the flat today, she thought.

'Do you live here alone?' She tried to sound casual in her turn, but there was a tell-tale quiver in her voice, she realised with vexation.

'I share with Tony Ericson, but he's in Zambia at the moment,' he returned laconically.

So although he might have a relationship with Karen Wellesley, they weren't actually living together. Briony experienced a spasm of relief at the realisation. She followed Logan into the living room. It wasn't large, and it was furnished in a spartan manner which suggested that its occupants spent little time there. The main items of furniture were a rather battered sofa drawn up in front of the fireplace and a large office desk in the window, supporting a litter of papers and two sturdy portable typewriters.

'Yes, I work here as well as at the office.' Logan deftly forestalled her next question. 'The kitchen is through the door opposite.' He pointed. 'Perhaps you'd like to make that coffee I mentioned while I have a shower.'

She was glad to have something to do. Filling the kettle and setting it to boil, and finding mugs and the jar of coffee occupied her hands, but did nothing to ease the mounting uncertainty within her. And she had no one to blame but herself for the current situation, she told herself, her shaking hands spilling coffee granules on to the worktop as she attempted to spoon them into the mugs. It was entirely of her own making. She'd followed Logan and thrown herself at his head, and if she turned and ran now, she would only be making an even bigger fool of herself. Yet if she stayed.... Briony's imagination refused to consider the implications of the next hour or two. She made the coffee and carried the mugs into the living room, but it was deserted. He was still in the shower, and now, if ever, was the time to beat an ignoble retreat. She set the mugs down on the corner of the desk and looked round for her bag. She'd put it down on the sofa as she'd come in, but it wasn't there. Nor was it on the desk, or on the floor, or on any of the shelves of the fitment which covered one wall, and housed books and a complicated-looking stereo player. It had vanished.

Or had she simply left it on the small table in the hall, she wondered desperately. She opened the living room door and peered out, but the table was bare except for the discarded envelopes from Logan's letters.

There was only one other explanation. Logan had taken her bag with him when he went off to have his shower, in order to prevent her from running out on him. The realisation set the match to her temper, relegating her fears and forebodings to a poor second. How dared he? she raged inwardly. She had taken several impetuous steps along the hall when one of the doors opened and Logan emerged, and the sight of him halted her dead in her tracks. He was wearing a damp towel hitched loosely round his hips, and his tawny hair was darkly streaked with water. His eyes, as they encountered Briony's openly hostile gaze, were enigmatic.

He said smoothly, 'Coming to meet me halfway, sweetheart?'

'I was coming to find my handbag.'

He gestured towards the door opposite him. 'It's in there.'

After only a second's hesitation, she turned and

walked into the room he had indicated. She had guessed it was his bedroom and she was right. Her bag was there, lying in the middle of the bed—a double bed, she registered in silence. There was little other furniture. Like the living room, it suggested that its occupant was someone constantly in transit, living out of suitcases, and there were few personal touches.

She picked her bag up from the bed, and turned. Logan was lounging in the doorway watching her, and she could read nothing from his expression, but his presence there meant that her retreat was effectively cut off.

'You didn't bring the coffee.' His tone was almost conversational.

'I—I didn't want any.' Damn! she thought in vexation. Why hadn't she said it was waiting in the living room, and thus made good her escape?

'Then I won't bother either,' he said affably, and walked forward. 'After all, why waste time when we have more important things to do?'

She took a step backwards. 'No,' she got out. 'I—I can't!'

'Can't you?' He didn't hurry as he covered the distance between them. He didn't have to. It wasn't a large room, and she was standing with her back against one wall. There was simply nowhere else to retreat to. 'You can,' he said. 'It's easy—I'll show you.'

He detached the bag from her suddenly nerveless fingers and tossed it on to a nearby chest of drawers, following it with her suit jacket which he slipped expertly from her shoulders, almost before she realised what he was doing, and then he was unfastening her shirt—as casually as if he was changing a dummy in a shop window, and with about as much feeling, she realised, a sense of hysteria rising deep within her. Her hands came up to push him away, her fingers fumbling as she sought to thrust the buttons he had undone back into their buttonholes.

'What's the matter?' He made no attempt to stop her. He was even smiling faintly.

'How dare you?' she choked.

'I wasn't aware that daring entered into it,' he said, his voice cool. 'You made it quite clear what you wanted, and I'm more than willing to provide it. So what's the problem?'

'The problem?' She stared at him helplessly. 'You're behaving as if—treating me like . . .'

'Like the spoiled brat you are?' he cut across her stumbling words with merciless harshness. 'What's the matter, darling! Isn't it all romantic enough for you? But what did you expect? It's ladies who are being seduced who get the flowers and champagne treatment. Little girls who throw themselves at men merely get laid. It may not be the lesson you expected to be taught this afternoon, but I hope it will prove a salutory one all the same. Now I suggest you get out of here before I forget you're your father's daughter and give you the beating you so richly deserve.'

For a minute she stared at him, then with a little inarticulate cry, she struck him across the face and ran past him out of the room and down the hall. She was struggling with the stiff catch on the front door when he caught her.

'You forgot your handbag.' His tone was soft and jeering. 'And your jacket.'

'Thank you.' She snatched at them, her face crimson with humiliation, suppressed tears stinging her eyelids.

Logan swore under his breath. 'Oh God, Briony!' He turned her to face him. 'You got off lightly,' he told her harshly. 'Just be thankful that I didn't take advantage of you, and for God's sake don't go round offering yourself to any other man who happens to take your schoolgirl fancy unless you want to end up as yet another unpleasant statistic for the sociologists to mull over.'

'Suddenly everyone feels they have a right to lecture me—to feel responsible for me,' she said stonily. 'Now please take your hands off me. I'd like to go home.'

He released her immediately. 'That's the best idea you've had yet.' He sounded weary. 'Go and play in your own league, sweetheart, and leave the adult games until such time as you've learned the rules.'

And the flat door slammed behind her.

The remembered sound seemed to strike an echo closer at hand, and Briony stirred in her chair, dragging herself almost reluctantly back from the pain of the past to the reality of the present. She soon saw what had roused her—the noise of a piece of coal falling out on to the hearth—and she knelt down to replace it on the fire and sweep up the resultant ash.

She was shocked when she glanced at her watch and saw how long she had been sitting there, remembering. A pointless exercise if ever there was one, she thought ironically. As she'd told Logan all those months ago, the past wasn't very productive. Only no one had warned her that the future could be even less so.

She got to her feet, stretching wearily. Now was the time to go and see about her room, otherwise she could well end up spending a cramped night in that very chair. But there was a surprise in store for her when she reached the top of the stairs and turned into the main bedroom at the front of the house. The bed was already made up and waiting, with crisply ironed sheets, and an old-fashioned eiderdown covered in flowered cotton.

Briony frowned as she set down her case and looked around her. Could it be possible that Aunt Hes was expected after all? But that was ridiculous, she knew. Aunt Hes rarely visited the cottage after the beginning of November, because she said frankly that the cold of North Yorkshire seemed to eat into her bones these days, apart from the fact that Kirkby Scar was often cut off by snow for days on end.

On the other hand, could she have let the cottage, perhaps? If so, when the tenant arrived, Briony would simply have to apologise and withdraw. She could spend a couple of days in York, she thought. Now that the tourist season was over, she would enjoy a leisurely tour of the Minster and the museums. It wasn't what she had planned, but was that necessarily a bad thing when most of the things she planned went so utterly and disastrously wrong?

She took a nightdress from her case and threw it across the bed, then walked to the window to draw the curtains. The second surprise was more in the nature of a shock. The darkness outside was full of the wild swirl of snowflakes, and the ground beneath as well as the kitchen roof and the neighbouring trees were already crusted in white. A swift sigh of exasperation escaped Briony's lips. She remembered now the forbidding leaden sky which had greeted her arrival, and realised she should have guessed its significance. She could still leave, of course. She could repack her case and find the car and drive to a slightly more accessible hotel. She glanced at her watch again, imagining the reaction if she turned up at this time of night without a booking. She might even end up spending the night in the car. No, she would stay where she was for tonight at least and risk being able to get out in the morning. It was surely too early in the winter for a really heavy fall, she argued to herself without a great deal of conviction. The real trouble was the isolation of the cottage from the village, and the difficulty of stocking up with fresh food if the weather was really turning nasty. She couldn't subsist for ever on a diet of black coffee.

They said everything came in threes, and the evening's surprises proved to be no exception. When she returned downstairs, the room was occupied. A large black cat with enormous green eyes was sitting in the middle of the hearthrug washing itself as if it had every right to be there. It turned its head gracefully as Briony came in and gave her a long speculative look before returning to its toilet.

Briony paused and watched it, her mouth curving upwards in amusement. Aunt Hes didn't own a cat, but she was probably notorious to the neighbouring feline population as a soft touch who could always be relied on for a saucer of milk, and this handsome beast had obviously realised the cottage was occupied again and drawn its own conclusions.

The only thing was—how had he got in? Briony went out into the hall again, but the front door was securely shut. She had opened no windows, so the cat must have got in via the kitchen. But how? Puzzled, she walked out into the kitchen and looked around. The back door was shut and the place was deserted, but someone had been in, presumably while she was upstairs, because a large cardboard box full of groceries now reposed in the centre of the kitchen table. A piece of folded notepaper was stuck in one side of the box and Briony unfolded it.

'Saw the car and thought I would bring these things up before the weather got worse,' she read. 'Hope all is satisfactory. Yours truly, N. Barnes.'

She looked into the box, her spirits lifting. Bread, butter, cartons of long-life milk, bacon and a couple of boxes of eggs. She wouldn't starve even if the blizzard outside raged for a week. But how had Mrs Barnes known? Perhaps she had simply seen the car parked at the foot of the track and decided to bring up some supplies. It could all be as simple as that, and Briony would take it for granted that was what had happened until she knew differently. Perhaps Mrs Barnes was naturally psychic, she thought grinning slightly to herself, as she unpacked the provisions and put them away. There was even a frozen chicken and a small joint of beef at the bottom of the box, so whoever was expected was apparently planning to stay.

The cat stalked into the kitchen and pushed itself against her legs, purring vociferously.

'Cupboard love,' Briony accused as she bent to fondle the glossy head. 'But we'll both have a drink in a minute.'

A hot milk drink for herself, she thought, and one of those tablets the doctor had prescribed for when she could not sleep, as something told her she would not do tonight. All this time she had survived by shutting out the past, refusing to admit its existence. Now she had allowed it back to torment her with a vengeance, and it was not done with her yet.

'Go and play in your own league,' Logan had said to her, she thought as she stood waiting for the milk to heat, and it was sound advice, although she had not realised it then. Christopher had been far more suitable in every way. Christopher who would be now telephoning vainly round all her friends in an effort to find out where she had gone. Christopher whom she had seriously been considering marrying until that unbelievable evening almost a week ago when she had gone to the head of the stairs, drawn there by the sound of her father's voice raised in anger, and seen Logan standing there. Logan who was dead—who'd been shot as a spy by Arab guerrillas. A much thinner Logan, his deeply tanned skin fine-drawn over his bones, lines of weariness etched around the grimness of his mouth as he stood quite immobile, his hands resting on his hips, his head bent slightly listening as her father raged at him.

She had heard herself cry out in disbelief, and they had both looked up at her—her father's face crimson with anger, Logan's eyes cool and cynical as they studied her in the long evening gown of midnight blue velvet, hanging sheer and straight to the floor.

He said, 'I've obviously picked a bad moment for my return from the grave. I'd like to see you some time, Briony, when you're less busy. And alone, preferably.'

And then he'd turned and gone out of the door into the night, and she'd taken one step towards him, her hand reaching out in a futile attempt to prevent his departure, her voice speaking his name, but perhaps it had been in silence, inside herself, because no sound had emerged, and then that strange stifling darkness had risen up and engulfed her.

She shuddered as she remembered the scene that awaited her when she had regained consciousness. Christopher had arrived by then for their evening's date and was standing there totally bewildered while Sir Charles raged on in the background. Her father, it seemed, blamed everyone, from the Azabian government who had allowed Logan to escape, down to the Foreign Office who had given no prior warning that he was alive and due back in the United Kingdom. If it hadn't been so horrible, it would almost have been funny.

'The infernal nerve of that swine—just turning up here like that!' Sir Charles fulminated, as Briony sat up, pushing away the glass of water that an anxious Mrs Lambert was trying to hold to her lips.

'Where else would he come?' she said. 'I am still his wife, after all.'

A fact that it was odd to acknowledge even to herself,

after almost a year of believing she was a widow, of trying to push to some distant recess of her mind all that happened in that brief, disastrous marriage because recriminations were useless now, because she would never be able to acknowledge the mistakes she had made. She had learned to live with all those realisations, and now her whole world had been turned upside down.

'But not for very much longer.' Sir Charles glared at her. 'Divorce proceedings can start right away. It isn't as if he hasn't given you grounds,' he added grimly.

'You really think it's as simple as that?' She stared up at him.

'Darling, it has to be.' Christopher moved to her side, his blue eyes troubled as he looked down at her. 'Face the facts. Your marriage was over before Logan went to Azabia. You left him—you can't deny that. He let you think he was dead. You can't intend just to let him walk back into your life as though nothing had happened.'

They had talked for the rest of the evening, while Briony sat in silence, her mind still trying to absorb the incredible thing which had happened to her. The doctor had called at her father's insistence, and administered a sedative, which she had not wanted. She needed to think, she had told herself. The sedative had been stronger than even she had imagined, and she had slept the clock round, to awake to a world that seemed blurred and slightly out of focus. She had dressed in a silk caftan and come downstairs to be told by Mrs Lambert that no one had called, no one had left a message. It began to seem that the events of the past twenty-four hours had all been some weird preposterous dream, but then the phone had begun to ring, and she had seen the front page stories in some of the newspapers littering the drawing room, and when she switched on the television Logan was there too, being interviewed on a news programme.

'But why,' the interviewer was asking him, 'did the Azabian terrorists announce that you were dead?'

Logan shrugged. 'Because they didn't want to admit that they'd been sloppy enough to allow me to escape, I suppose. They'd intended to kill me, and when I got away they were furious. They put a fair price on my head, and I think it's proof of the unpopularity of the new régime that so many people were willing to hide me and help me out of the country in spite of the money being offered.'

'Your escape took a long time.'

'Indeed it did. I had to remain in hiding sometimes for weeks at a time because there were troops looking for me. If I'd been found, I would have been shot and so would those who were helping me, so I had to be extra careful.'

'And there was no possibility of informing the British authorities that you were safe?'

'None,' Logan said. 'I'd been one of the last Western correspondents left in Azabia as it was, and all the Embassy staff had been evacuated months before. I had to wait until I crossed the border before I could let anyone know where I was.'

'And even then you didn't let it be generally known that you were alive after all. Can you tell us why that was?'

'Personal reasons,' said Logan.

'Can it have been that you wanted to avoid if possible the inevitable ballyhoo that would result when it was known you had escaped?' the interviewer pressed him.

Logan gave a quick tight smile. 'If I did, then it hasn't worked,' he said with a swift gesture at the cameras and microphones.

'With the story that you have to tell, I would imagine

that you're in the line for another Journalist of the Year award. You will be returning to your staff job on the *Courier?*'

'Perhaps. You could say my plans are fluid at the moment.' For a moment Logan stared straight at the camera, and Briony had the oddest feeling that he was looking straight at her. She got up in one swift movement and turned off the set.

That evening the pressure began again. She found that her father had invited not only Christopher to have dinner with them, but also George Forrester, their family solicitor. It was like some strange council of war, she thought almost hysterically, as she listened to Mr Forrester carefully outlining the grounds for divorce under the current laws, and the time period that would elapse before she could hope to be free. Her father was nodding resignedly and Christopher was patting her hand, and it was a surprise to hear herself say, 'Will you all please stop talking about me as if I didn't exist!'

Sir Charles said brusquely, 'Briony, you're overwrought, and no wonder. Go and lie down, my dear. We'll discuss this with you later, when you're feeling calmer.'

'I'm perfectly calm! And if my life, my future is being discussed, I think I have a right to be included in the discussions.'

'But you're still a child,' her father declared angrily. 'You're no more fit to decide what's best for you now than you were when you married that man.'

She said drily, 'On the contrary, I don't even think I'm the same person. Probably Logan isn't either. We could be two strangers meeting.'

The milk boiled over and Briony rushed to its rescue, the word 'strangers' beating in her brain. She and Logan had never been anything but strangers, she thought achingly, and nor, it seemed, would they ever be. Deliberately, she thrust the last, most hurtful memory away from her. She wouldn't think about that now.

She poured what was left of the milk into a beaker and added some drinking chocolate to it. She switched off the kitchen lamp, and placed the guard carefully in front of the fire before turning off the living room lamps. The cat had vanished, but she was not altogether surprised when she arrived upstairs to find it curled into a sleek coil on her bed.

'The nerve of you!' she said aloud, but she was smiling and the cat made not the slightest attempt to move. It was cold upstairs, and Briony was glad to put her housecoat on over her nightdress as she made her way to the tiny bathroom, which Aunt Hes had converted out of the third and smallest bedroom, to wash and clean her teeth. There was a rubber hot water bottle hanging on a hook near the basin, and she filled it, hugging it to her as she walked back along the narrow landing to her room.

Her hand was on the landing light switch when she heard from the hall below the unmistakable sound of a key being turned in the front door. For a moment her knees turned to water as she stood there, then common sense reasserted itself. If the late night visitor had a key, then he or she had a right to be entering the cottage. It would be, inevitably, this unknown tenant of Aunt Hes's, Briony told herself ruefully, tightening the sash on her housecoat, whose food she had begun to eat, and in whose nicely aired bed she had been proposing to retire. She would have to apologise humbly and do a quick rethink.

The front door opened and a blast of icy wind filled the narrow hallway, together with a few odd snowflakes. The shadow that came in was tall and distinctly masculine in shape, and Briony groaned inwardly. It would have been far simpler to have explained to a woman, she thought.

She peered down the stairs and saw that the shadow had turned into a graven image. Riveted to the spot, no doubt, she thought, by letting himself into an empty house to find a woman in a housecoat looking embarrassed at the top of the stairs. She began to hunt round for an appropriate phrase to begin the explanations and apologies, then the hall light clicked on and the words shrivelled and died on her lips as she looked down into the face of the man standing below her.

For a moment, they stood in silence staring at each other.

Then, 'Hello, wife,' said Logan with no expression in his voice whatsoever.

CHAPTER THREE

'You—what are you doing here?' High-pitched and frightened, it didn't even sound like her own voice.

Logan put down the suitcase and the portable typewriter he was carrying.

'I could ask you the same thing,' he said evenly.

'Where did you get the key from?' she demanded.

'From your aunt, four days ago, just before she left for the South of France.' He raised his eyebrows. 'What's your story?'

'I used the spare key. The one that's kept under the broken stone.'

'So.' He uttered a short, totally mirthless laugh. 'Here we are, then.'

'No, we're not,' she said between her teeth. 'I'm getting out, right now.'

'Like that?' The cool aquamarine eyes raked her dispassionately. 'You'll be a sensation. And you're going nowhere.'

'You can't stop me!'

'I don't even propose to try,' he said indifferently. 'But the weather will. Was that snow-covered lump I passed at the bottom of the track your car, by any chance?'

Briony suppressed an exclamation. 'Is it that bad?'

'It's that bad,' he said laconically, 'and it's going to get worse. I left my car on the other side of the village and walked the last few miles.'

'Then I can do the same.'

'My God,' he said wearily, 'then you really are a fool.'

'How did you know I was here?'

'I didn't.' It was a grim statement. 'Your aunt played a neat trick on us both. I don't know what she's hoping for.'

Briony felt a flush stealing into her cheeks. 'As a matter of fact ...'

'Yes?' he prompted as she hesitated.

'As a matter of fact, she didn't know I was coming here. I knew she'd be away and that the place would be empty. I wanted to be on my own for a while. No one knows that I'm here.'

'Well, that's just hard lines, I'm afraid,' he said. 'And the place isn't empty. It's being occupied—by me, unlike you, with your aunt's permission. I'm renting it from her.'

Briony sagged helplessly against the wall. 'But for how long?'

'As long as it takes.' He shrugged. 'I've been commissioned to write a book about my experiences in escaping from Azabia. I've come here to rough out the first draft.

That's why I wanted some peace and quiet.'

'And you'll have it,' she said. 'Maybe not tonight, but first thing in the morning I'll be away and gone from here.'

Logan's mouth twisted cynically. 'I wouldn't bank on it, sweetheart.' He shrugged off the leather car coat he was wearing. 'Your aunt said she'd make sure there were some stores in the place. Have they come, do you know?'

'Everything's in the kitchen. I—I put them away. I had no idea who they were for.'

'Naturally,' he agreed wearily. 'It's all an amazing coincidence, isn't it, Briony? Like the time you followed me to that pub for lunch. Like the time you came round to the flat with those cuttings I'd asked for after I got back from Cambodia.'

'You mean'—for a moment words failed her—'You think I came here deliberately—knowing that you were going to be here? You must be out of your mind!'

'No,' he said. 'I've merely given up trying to figure what goes on in yours. Now if you'll excuse me I'll go and make myself a hot drink.' He disappeared through the door leading into the living room.

Briony hesitated for a minute, then picking up the skirts of her housecoat she came down the stairs and followed him into the kitchen. He was standing at the sink filling the kettle, and he shot a look at her over his shoulder.

'What's this? Wifely solicitude? It's a little late for that, isn't it?'

'Very probably.' She moistened her dry lips with the tip of her tongue. 'Logan, what are we going to do? We can't both stay here—it's impossible under the circumstances.'

'I don't see why.' He put the kettle on the stove. 'We're legally married. We're allowed to share a roof, even if we haven't been in the habit of doing so. And you have my word for it that's all we'll share—just in case you were harbouring any delusions that I still lust after that expensively packaged little carcase of yours.'

'It's no wonder you're a journalist, Logan,' she said with gritted teeth. 'You really have a way with words!'

'Ain't it the truth, lady?' He gave her a derisive look. 'And I'm not a journalist any more—at least not with the *Courier*. My services have been dispensed with, to poor Mac's everlasting disgust—and we know whom we have to thank for that, don't we?'

Mortification at her father's sheer vindictiveness kept her silent.

Eventually she said, 'I don't know what to say.'

'Don't you? If this snow keeps up, you'll have plenty of opportunity to think of something. But I'm afraid you'll have to talk to yourself. I came here for some peace. I can't work in London. The bloody phone never stops, for one thing. Suddenly they want me to appear on chat shows. My God,' he laughed shortly, 'instant fame!'

'It isn't a very large cottage,' she said coldly. 'But I'll do my best to keep out of your way.'

'Thank you.' He made her a slight, mocking bow. 'What a pity you haven't got the fells to escape to this time. What a sensation for the locals if history were to repeat itself!' He spooned coffee into a mug and filled it with boiling water. 'I've wondered sometimes, Briony, what would have happened that day if I hadn't rushed off full of romantic ardour to fetch some champagne to toast you in—if I'd been here to head that Chapman bitch off. I've wondered if our—marriage, for want of a better word would have followed a different pattern.'

'I doubt it,' said Briony, conscious that her heart was

hammering oddly. 'And it's a singularly fruitless form of speculation.'

'You think so?' He drank some of the coffee. 'Yet it came into my mind quite often when I was locked up in that stinking jail—and afterwards when I was on the run. The curiosity of leaving a house with everything in the world to return to, then coming back half an hour later to find that in fact you have nothing. Nothing at all.' He smiled reflectively. 'An odd sensation, to say the least.'

There was a silence. Briony stared down at the stone flags, unwilling to look up and meet his gaze.

She said, trying to control her uneven breathing, 'I know where Aunt Hes keeps the extra bedding. I'll put some in front of the fire to air for a while. I'm afraid I'm using the bed Mrs Barnes made up for you.'

He said, 'There's no need to bother about extra bedding—at least tonight.' He threw up one hand, his lips twisting satirically, as she looked up in swift alarm. 'And no need for panic either. I'll make do with a couple of chairs down here for what's left of the night. I've slept in worse places, believe me, over the past few months.'

Somewhere inside her a little demon whispered, 'And in the past few days—where have you slept? In Karen Wellesley's bed?' But she did not ask the question.

Logan said with sudden impatience, 'Oh, get to bed, for God's sake, Briony. Lock the door if you want—and if you can't take my word for it that rape isn't imminent.'

A gust of anger shook her. 'I wouldn't take your word for what day of the week it is!'

'It's Tuesday,' he said inimically. 'But something tells me that knowing the names is going to assume less importance in our lives than simply getting through them, one by one. Now get out of here.'

It wasn't until she was safely in her room with the door closed that Briony realised she was still clutching the rubber hot water bottle. It had lost much of its initial heat too, she thought ruefully, but she was reluctant to venture back to the bathroom and risk encountering Logan again.

She slipped out of her housecoat and got into bed with a shiver. She could hear slight sounds of movement from downstairs, and tried to close her ears to them. No matter what he might say, what assurances he might give, she was going to do her level best to get out of here in the morning. It was a terrible, malicious fate which had driven Logan and herself to seek the same refuge, but she was not obliged to succumb to it.

She twisted and turned, punching the pillow into shape, trying to relax and get comfortable, but it was impossible. Out of the darkness, she kept seeing Logan's face, frozen with shock as he registered her presence at the top of the stairs, and the bitter irony of his words, 'Hello, wife.'

They'd been the first words he'd spoken to her at the start of their honeymoon in this very cottage. The first words of love—and the last. Just after that he'd gone off—to fetch some champagne as he'd said—and by the time he'd returned she had gone, running out on to the fells like a mad thing, running from the things that Marina Chapman had screamed at her, from the poison and the hatred which had struck at the very roots of her love for him.

Love? she thought wryly. Looking back, it now seemed more of an obsession. Logan had not been unfair when he had suggested she might have pursued him here. She supposed that after his rejection of her at the flat, he had expected she would never want to see him or speak to him again, but he had been wrong.

She had returned home, hurt and humiliated, to find Sir Charles waiting for her grimly. She had, of course, been seen on her abortive visit to the U.P.G. offices and Sir Charles had lost no time in instigating enquiries as to exactly what his daughter had been doing there. The answers had not pleased him. And apart from that, he wanted to know where she had been since then.

Briony, still on edge over her treatment at Logan's hands, answered him hotly, and before long a full-scale row was in progress. Hard things were said on both sides and the culmination came when Briony stalked out of the room, declaring that she was leaving.

An hour later she was sitting in the kitchen of Aunt Hes's comfortable mews flat, swearing that she would never return.

Aunt Hes heard her out in a troubled silence. She had never liked her brother-in-law, but she had always taken a great deal of trouble not to interfere.

She said, 'But my dear, you have nowhere to go, and no money except the allowance your father makes you. What are you going to do?'

Briony said with determination, 'Well, the first thing I must do is find a job of some kind.'

'Have you any idea what?'

'I thought I might apply to the Personnel Director at U.P.G. I have it on good authority that there are usually vacancies there.'

Aunt Hes frowned slightly. 'My dear, is that wise?'

'Probably not, but I don't want to be wise.' Briony's tone was defiant. 'Everything I've ever done has been safely mapped out for me, with no margin for error. Well, I want to learn by my mistakes the same as other girls do.'

'As your mother did,' her aunt observed, half to herself.

Briony leaned forward. 'You never would tell me before,' she said. 'Was—was my mother happy with Daddy?'

'She loved him.' Hester Wyatt's voice was dry. 'That, I understand, is supposed to confer a kind of happiness.'

'But did it?' Briony persisted.

'If it did not,' Aunt Hes said slowly, 'then your mother was too loyal ever to discuss the alternative. But I wondered—I wondered very much. She was impulsive like you,' she added.

Briony's eyes softened. 'I wish I could remember her properly.'

'I wish you could. I wish she was here now to stop you careering headlong to disaster,' her aunt said vigorously.

'What's so disastrous about leaving home and getting a job?' Briony gave her aunt a limpid smile. 'Girls do it every day.'

'It wasn't that I was thinking of.' Aunt Hes gave her a straight look. 'It was the rest of the story—the part you haven't told me.'

'I don't know what you mean.' Briony looked down at the floor, avoiding her aunt's gaze, and heard her give a swift sigh.

'Keep your secret, child,' she said, after a moment's pause. 'But be discreet. Your father is a bad man to cross. I'm going up to Kirkby Scar for a few days, so if you want to use the flat, you may. Wasn't that really what you came to ask?'

'Oh, lord!' Briony had the grace to look slightly amused. 'Am I that transparent?'

Aunt Hes got up to clear the coffee cups, and patted her cheek affectionately. 'You're your mother's daughter,' she said. 'And she was my only sister, after all. I knew her rather well. I knew the look when she was about to ask some outrageous favour—and I knew when she was about to embark on some new love affair that she thought I wouldn't approve of. But in your case, it's not my approval that matters, it's your father's. I appeal to you, Briony, be careful.'

Aunt Hes's warning was still ringing in Briony's ears forty-eight hours later, as she became U.P.G.'s latest recruit for the cutting library. She had no illusions about the job. She was a dogsbody, pure and simple, signing files full of cuttings on every subject under the sun in and out of a large book kept for the purpose, supplying background information on any subject required to the various editorial departments, and tracking files that had gone missing. The head of the department was a Miss Johnson, an elderly Gorgon, round whom even editors trod warily, and juniors as a rule did not stay more than a few weeks, Briony was rather wearily informed by her immediate superior Jenny Braithwaite.

'La Johnson chews them up and spits them out,' she explained, during Briony's first coffee break in the canteen. 'Although perhaps she'll make an exception in your case.'

'I don't think so.' Briony had already encountered the formidable Miss Johnson and suffered a tongue-lashing from her over a file that had not been returned to its correct place on the bulging shelves of the library. The person who had returned the file had hardly had time to leave the room before the tirade began, and Briony suspected that Miss Johnson had orders from above to lean on her.

She had telephoned her father the previous night and told him she had persuaded Personnel to give her a chance, and to her surprise he had accepted her news almost genially, at the same time letting her see that he didn't believe she would be able to hold the job down.

After a couple of hours with Miss Johnson, she knew exactly what he was getting at, but her determination hardened. She would not be driven out no matter how unfair the treatment might be. She would not return home with her tail between her legs, confessing her fault, and asking to be taken back into the fold like a black sheep. She had as much right to carve out a life for herself as anyone else.

She had naturally expected she would see Logan again quite soon and nerved herself inwardly for the inevitable confrontation, but it was not to take place, she discovered with a strange chagrin, at least not at once. Logan was abroad again, and no one was altogether sure when he would be back, or what he was actually doing, although he was said to be in the Far East. Though she scanned the *Courier* every day, Briony saw no stories filed under his byline.

In the meantime she began to settle to the routine of her work better than she could ever have expected. Miss Johnson, she realised, would never change, but she liked Jenny and got on well with her, and guessed that they might have become friends, perhaps even flatmates, if Briony had not been Sir Charles Trevor's daughter. As it was, no matter how many breaks and lunches she and Jenny might share there was always an invisible barrier there, which Briony regretted.

She had been working at U.P.G. for three weeks when her father telephoned her at the flat to say that he was going to the States for a few weeks on business.

'I hope by the time I return you will have got this nonsense out of your head once and for all, Briony,' he said coldly, before he rang off.

Nonsense! Briony thought with an inward sigh, as she laid her own receiver back on the rest. That was what her father thought of her bid for independence, of her attempt to earn her own living. She supposed it had its amusing side, but she was damned if she could see what it was at that particular moment.

She had to start making other plans for herself anyway. Aunt Hes would be returning soon from Kirkby Scar. Her aunt had been a widow for a number of years and had become a successful writer of children's books, but she made no bones about needing solitude for her work, either in London or Yorkshire, and Briony suspected she would be dismayed to find her niece still in occupation when she returned. It had after all been planned only as a temporary arrangement. She wondered again about Jenny, who she knew shared a flat with two other girls. Would they have room for a fourth? she wondered rather dispiritedly. And would they even want her? Or she could always contact one of her former schoolmates, she supposed reluctantly.

She was still in this indecisive state when she went to work the next day and learned quite by chance that Logan had returned. It was Miss Johnson of all people who gave her the news, tutting angrily as she entered the cuttings library.

'I do not approve of files going out of the building,' she was muttering, opening and closing the drawers of her desk with little slams, an idiosyncrasy of hers which Briony had noticed before when she was upset. 'I do not approve. And of course none of the messengers can be spared. They'll have to go in a taxi—there's nothing else for it. A complete waste of time and money!'

She glanced up and caught Briony watching her in some surprise.

'Get on with your work,' she snapped.

'I've finished, actually.' Briony spoke with some reluctance, knowing the admission was likely to lead to some foul and unnecessary cross-indexing task.

'I see.' Miss Johnson tapped a pencil against her teeth. 'Then I suppose you will have to do. One of the foreign news reporters on the *Courier* is just back from Cambodia, and he wants all the background files taking round to his flat, if you please, and Mr Mackenzie who one would have thought would have known better has actually authorised it.'

Briony's heartbeat seemed to be behaving in a strange, unpredictable manner.

'Which of the reporters?'

Miss Johnson stared at her frostily. 'Logan Adair—if it matters,' she snapped. 'My concern is the inconvenience to this department. You'd better look out the necessary files and take them round at once. Get a receipt for the taxi fare and claim it at the cashier's desk when you return.' She glanced at her watch and her mouth set in resentment. 'I suppose there'll be barely time for you to get back before the office closes. When you've delivered the files, you may go home. But be punctual in the morning,' she added hastily, as if afraid that this concession on her part might lead to excesses of tardiness on Briony's. She would have been shocked to the core if she had known that the most junior member of her department was not listening to a word that she was saying.

Briony's hands were shaking as she sought out the files, and even when she was actually sitting in the taxi which was taking her to Logan's flat, she found it difficult to believe that it was all really happening. Inwardly, she was shaking like a leaf. And yet there was no reason why she should be nervous, she told herself. She was simply doing a job, that was all. Heavens, she hadn't even angled for the chance to take the files to Logan's flat. And though she could tell herself that he had probably forgotten completely the circumstances of their last disastrous encounter, she had not.

Outside the door of the flat, she took a deep breath, then rang the bell. There was a prolonged silence. For a moment she thought it had all been a mistake and that there was no one there, and she experienced a pang of something which hovered between regret and relief. She was on the point of turning away when she heard a sound inside the flat and the door swung open.

Logan was standing there, and her first thought was that he looked ghastly. He was pale under his tan, and his eyes were over-bright and slightly bloodshot as if he was suffering from a fever. They narrowed slightly in disbelief as he looked her over.

'What the hell are you doing here?' His voice was hardly encouraging, and the words were slightly slurred.

'I brought these.' She held out the files, and he stared down at them as if he was having difficulty in focussing, or even recognising what they were.

'You brought them? You?'

'Yes. I work at U.P.G. now—in the cuttings library. No one else was free to bring these, so I was sent.' She could hear herself stammering a little, aware that her colour had heightened.

'God in heaven!' Logan leaned against the door jamb and shook his head as if he was trying to clear it.

'You're not well,' she said, all her concern aroused. 'Let me come in.'

'I'm perfectly well.' He pushed the hair back from his forehead with an irritated gesture. 'And I'm in no mood for a social call.'

'It isn't a social call,' she protested, her anxious eyes searching his face, taking in his haggard expression, the shadows beneath his eyes, the lines which had deepened beside his mouth. 'You're ill. You need a doctor. Let me . . .'

He gave a jeering laugh. 'I need to finish this piece I'm

writing on Cambodia, my dear Miss Nightingale, and for that I need another drink—several drinks, in fact, not medical attention.'

He turned away abruptly and left her standing on the doorstep. She watched him move away, his steps betraying only the slightest unsteadiness as he walked down the passage, and after a brief hesitation she followed, closing the front door behind her.

He was standing by the desk in the sitting room when she went in. The desk top was littered with paper, and the typewriter stood open, a half-completed piece of copy in its rollers. Beside it stood a half-empty bottle of whisky and a used glass. The air was stale and reeked of cigarette smoke. Briony grimaced, and walking to the window pushed the lower sash up a few inches, permitting some welcome fresh air to enter the room.

'Make yourself at home,' Logan suggested grittily.

'You need some black coffee.' She set the cuttings files down on the desk and went towards the kitchen.

'I've told you what I bloody need,' he said savagely. 'And it isn't your ministrations for a kick-off. Now for God's sake, get out and leave me in peace!'

She glanced round the disordered room. 'I like your idea of peace,' she said coolly. 'It isn't mine.'

'But then so few of our ideas coincide,' he mocked. 'Go home, Briony. I don't want you here.' He grabbed the sheet of paper out of the typewriter and screwed it into a ball, hurling it to the ground with a muttered obscenity.

'You need someone,' she retorted. 'How long is it since you last ate?'

'I don't remember. Does it matter?'

'Of course it does! No wonder you're awash with whisky on an empty stomach. I'll make you some scrambled egg.'

'God,' he muttered under his breath. Then, 'If I eat your bloody eggs will you go?'

'We'll see.' She slipped off her jacket and tossed it on to the sofa. She found eggs and butter in the kitchen, and washed the pan she proposed to use. The eggs were as near perfection as she had ever managed, fluffy and creamy, and she felt a flicker of pride as she spooned them on to the waiting rounds of crisp toast.

Logan was typing when she re-entered the sitting room, his entire concentration fixed on the words forming on the paper in front of him. He hardly seemed aware of her presence as she stood beside him holding the tray.

At last she ventured, 'Logan—you must eat.'

He said curtly, 'Leave it somewhere. I'll eat it later.'

'It will spoil,' she began to protest, then, reading the anger in his face, she capitulated, setting the tray down on a table by the sofa. She sat down, watching him, sensing that at that moment he was being driven by something she did not and never would understand.

It was a relief when he ripped the sheet out of the machine and laid it down. Almost abstractedly, he reached out for a fork and she put the food within his reach as he read over what he had written. Briony realised suddenly she was holding her breath, and made herself relax, chiding herself inwardly for being foolish.

'It's all right,' Logan muttered at last, as he laid down his knife and fork.

'The story or the food?'

'Both, I guess.' His mouth twisted wryly. 'Thanks for your contribution.' He picked up the page of copy and looked at it. 'I think I've managed to strike the happy medium—to tell enough of the truth without putting the sensitive readers of the *Courier* off their bacon and eggs, which would never do.'

'What do you mean?'

'Let me explain. When I get back from some stinking, bleeding hell-hole in the world as I did last night, I write two stories—one for me, telling it like it is—as if I could forget. God, sometimes I wish I could! Then I produce an edited version, suitable for the family breakfast table of millions. Just enough for people to say, "What a terrible thing. What is the world coming to?" but not enough for them to throw their guts up as I did when they took me round that children's hospital.' He reached for the whisky bottle and poured another measure into his glass.

'Don't you think you've had enough?' Briony asked unhappily.

'No, my sweet, I do not think so. In fact I've only just begun. Now that the story's finished, I intend to get smashed out of my mind.'

'Is that wise?'

'Perhaps not, my lovely innocent, but bloodly necessary, believe me. Cheers.' He lifted the glass in a mock toast. 'Can you suggest a better way of blotting out my memories of the past few weeks so they don't return to give me nightmares?'

She shook her head silently, registering the depths of bitterness and revulsion she heard in his voice.

Logan tossed back the whisky with a practised flick of the wrist and refilled the glass.

'What's the matter, Miss Trevor? You look disturbed.' The mockery was back in his tone. 'Is it a shock to find that journalists have feelings too? That we can't look on the dead, the half-dead, and those who ought to be dead and remain unmoved? That we aren't altogether the vicious, sub-human stratum of society that your father would have you believe?'

'You aren't being fair!'

'I'm not feeling particularly fair,' he returned

brusquely. He flicked the files she had brought with his finger. 'You can return these as soon as you like, messenger girl.'

'It will have to be in the morning,' she said. 'I've finished for the day.'

His brows lifted and he glanced down at his watch. 'So you have. How time does fly when one's enjoying oneself! Well, good evening, Miss Trevor. Don't let me keep you from the social whirl. Or hasn't Daddy got a prize-giving for you to attend tonight?'

'I'm not living at home any more. I—I have a flat. And my father's in the States. Anything more you would like to know?'

His mouth twisted. 'You have been busy while I've been away,' he remarked. 'What sparked off this sudden urge for emancipation?'

Briony was tempted to reply, 'You did,' but held her tongue.

'You really think of me as a child,' she said slowly at last, her tone clouded by disappointment and bewilderment.

'I try not to think of you at all.' Logan leaned back in his chair, closing his eyes wearily. 'It makes life much simpler.'

'Why?'

'It's not important!' He shook his head and reached for his glass again.

'You've had enough to drink,' she said. 'Logan—please ...'

'Logan, please,' he mimicked unpleasantly. 'Just what the hell gives you the right to consider yourself my keeper?'

'The fact that I care about you. That I care what happens to you,' she said fiercely.

'Am I supposed to be grateful for that?' he lashed

back. 'We're strangers, Miss Trevor, ships that pass in the night. Let's keep it that way.'

'You mean I have a choice?' she enquired forlornly. 'Why the hostility, Logan? What have I done?'

'Nothing, love, nothing.' He raised the glass to his lips and drank reflectively. 'You exist, that's all, and sometimes I tend to be too aware of the fact for my own peace of mind.'

'Careful, Mr Adair!' It was her turn to mock. 'That sounds dangerously like an admission.'

He smiled cynically. 'Well, don't build on it, Miss Trevor.'

'Why not? You made it clear more than once that you found me attractive, so why do I have to be shut out of your life so completely?' She tried to smile. 'Nothing heavy, Logan—but why?'

'Because it's better that way.' He studied the remains of the whisky in his glass as if he was preparing a chemical analysis of it. 'Do I really have to enumerate the reasons? One—I'm too old for you. Two—your father may pay my salary, but he hates me and everything I stand for. Three—you don't know me, or anything about me. We don't just inhabit different worlds, but different planets. Need I go on?'

'Yes—if you intend to convince me.' Tell me about Karen Wellesley, she thought. Tell me that she's your woman, and that she's all you want, and then I'll go. I'll be glad to go before I make an even bigger fool of myself than I've done already.

He said slowly, 'What if I were to tell you that ever since I threw you out that afternoon, I've been kicking myself. At the time, I regarded it as one of the few chivalrous gestures of my life, now I tend to think that chivalry might better be confined to eunuchs. Perhaps they could cope with the consequences of it better than

I have.' He got to his feet. 'Come here, Briony.'

She went slowly, standing in front of him submissively. She had never felt so gauche or so unsure, but when his arms went round her she clung to him, closing her eyes, offering him her parted lips. He wasn't gentle, but his desire for her stopped just short of brutality, and she felt something wild and unknown deep within her respond to him. Whatever he'd have asked, she would have given gladly, unthinkingly, there and then, on the dusty carpet in the cluttered room, if that was what he wanted. She had never dreamed that such a need could exist, or that it could be mutual. He was whispering her name as his mouth restlessly caressed her eyelids, her temples, her cheeks, the lobes of her ears, before returning to plunder her mouth again.

'You taste as good as you smell,' he said huskily at last, his hands tangled in her hair, as he regarded her, the aquamarine eyes hooded and slightly enigmatic.

'It's Givenchy,' she said inanely, and felt a quiver of amusement go through him.

'Naturally,' he said gravely. 'And this is—madness.' His voice sank to a whisper as he lowered his head towards her again, lifting her into his arms and carrying her towards the sofa. This time she made no protest as he began to unfasten the shirt she was wearing, his lips lazily following the path of his hands.

'You're beautiful,' he murmured at last. 'And you don't need this.' Her bra joined her discarded shirt on the floor beside them. 'Perfect.' His hands were gentle on her as if he knew this was the first time she had yielded herself to so intimate a caress. 'Like half-opened flowers—rosebuds.' His lips teased her erotically, rousing her unawakened breasts to full bloom, drowning her in a sensual dream from which she had no wish to recover. The dingy surroundings had faded, and the only reality was the deepening pressure of Logan's body against hers, and his hands moving on her softly as he began to rid her of the rest of her clothes.

When a door banged, it might have been in a different world. But the footsteps that were coming down the passage were real enough, and so was the door opening violently, and the laughing male voice exclaiming, 'So you're back, you bastard, are you ... Oh, God!'

The sitting room door slammed shut. Logan jack-knifed into a sitting position, cursing under his breath.

'Who was that?' Briony pressed her hands to suddenly burning cheeks. The intruder might not have seen everything, but he would have had more than a shrewd idea of what was going on.

'Tony. I share the flat with him.' Logan got to his feet, straightening his own clothing. 'He wasn't due back until tomorrow, damn it, or I'd have taken the precaution of locking the door at least. We make a point of not intruding on each other when we're—entertaining. It's worked very well—until this evening.' He saw her looking at him and swore softly. 'Don't look like that, Briony. You must have known—you can't have believed you were the first one.'

'Of course not!' She huddled into the garments he had removed with such tender skill—a lifetime ago?—avoiding his gaze.

'And if he did recognise you, he can be persuaded to keep his mouth shut, if that's what's worrying you.' Logan's mouth twisted cynically.

'It isn't.' Which wasn't strictly true, she realised. It had taken her only one horrified moment after Tony's retreat to realise the sidelong looks and muttered gossip which could be waiting for her at U.P.G. the following day. And it would be bound to get back to her father. She knew it.

But the really shattering realisation was that she had come within seconds of allowing herself to be seduced by a man she hardly knew, and that she would not have simply permitted such an occurrence but wanted it with all her body and soul and mind. Without Tony's interruption, she would have belonged completely to Logan by now and she knew it.

'Briony.' His voice was gentler than she had ever heard it, and his hands clasped her face, forcing her to look up at him. 'It's all right. Everything's all right. Nothing happened to you. Don't hate me, and for God's sake don't start hating yourself.'

'I—don't hate you.' Her voice broke, and he kissed her trembling lips.

'That's good.' He was smiling, but his eyes were troubled. 'Don't worry about getting out of here. I'll call you a cab, and Tony will be lying low in his room while you get clear.'

'You're turning me out?' She could hardly believe her own words. Where was her pride? she asked herself wildly as humiliated colour stained her cheeks.

'As a temporary measure.' He went over to the desk and handed her a memo pad and a pencil. 'Write your flat number down and I'll call you there tomorrow.'

'But Logan ...'

'There are no "buts". At least, not tonight. It's not just Tony's return, you know.' He pushed a rueful hand through his hair. 'I've probably got too much whisky in my bloodstream to do justice to either of us.'

'It was so dreadful,' she whispered. 'Him bursting in like that.'

'He feels dreadful too. He's probably contemplating suicide at this very moment.'

'That's not true,' she said passionately. 'In spite of your early warning system, I'm not the first he's caught you with. You more or less said so yourself?'

'I think a discussion of what may or may not have happened in the past is pretty fruitless right now. I'll take you home.' Logan went back to the desk, lifted the telephone and dialled a number.

Briony said stiffly, 'It's all right. You don't have to come with me.'

'Yes, I do.' He ordered their taxi and replaced the receiver. He said, 'I'm not going to touch you, Briony. I'm not even coming near you while I say this. But you're not just any girl, and I wasn't making a drunken pass because you were there and available. We could have something quite different going for us, and that's why I'm glad that I'm taking you home now, and that I'll be phoning you tomorrow when I'm sober and thinking straight again. Perhaps you'd better do some hard thinking too, or you might suddenly find you were right in, out of your depth.'

She said with difficulty, her eyes filling with tears. 'I think I love you, Logan.'

He did not move. He stayed where he was, leaning against the desk, and his mouth twisted a little.

He said lightly, 'You catch on fast, Miss Trevor. Just be sure that you're waiting by that phone tomorrow evening.'

Looking back on the period that followed, Briony supposed she had never been happier in her life. Logan telephoned her as he promised and took her out to dinner. But he made no further attempt to seduce her either then or on any of the other evenings which followed. She saw him at work too, and whenever possible he took her to lunch with him. She knew that everyone in the office was speculating about them, and she knew too that with her father due home from the States any day their romance was living on borrowed time. She had half expected a scene with Karen Wellesley, but apart from giving her venomous looks on any occasion when they happened to encounter each other, the older woman ignored Briony completely.

And Aunt Hes returned from Yorkshire, her head humming, as she herself said, with a new plot. She told Briony warmly that she was looking well, and was welcome to stay on at the flat for as long as she wanted, but Briony knew that as soon as her aunt began writing in earnest she would be in the way. She would have to find somewhere else to live.

She supposed she could go home. Word had reached U.P.G. that Sir Charles was delayed in the States, and no one seemed exactly sure when he would be returning.

'Or I could move in with you,' she said to Logan mischievously one night as they sat together in Aunt Hes's drawing room, listening to records. 'I hear Tony's going back to Africa next week.'

'You hear altogether too much.' His tone was short, and he sat up abruptly, dislodging her from where she had been dreaming with her head on his shoulder.

Briony was taken aback. 'It was only a joke,' she began.

'Not an amusing one. I've never lived with a woman in my life, and I don't intend to start now. It wouldn't be fair.'

'On whom?' she asked rather indignantly.

'On anyone involved,' he snapped. 'But particularly unfair to the girl. You've said yourself that Tony's going abroad again next week. God knows where I'll be sent next, now I've finished that series of articles on Cambodia, or when, even. I could be away next week myself. And what would you do then? Stay on at the flat and see which of us comes back first—Tony or myself?'

She gasped, 'That's a foul thing to say!'

'Well, it's a foul idea. I share the flat with Tony because it suits us both, because of the sort of life we lead. But it's not an arrangement which could be stretched to include a woman. It would lead to all sorts of problems.'

'But surely,' she stared at him, 'you and Tony—you'll get married one day—one of you, or both.'

Logan shrugged. 'Doubtful. Journalism isn't the life for a married man. I've seen too many marriages crack up because the girl never knew from one day to the next where her husband was or what he was doing.'

'I see.' Briony got up from the sofa. 'I'd better see about some coffee. Aunt Hes will be home from the theatre soon.'

Logan said wearily, 'There's time enough for that. Come back here, Briony. Look at me.' His gaze narrowed as it rested on her face. 'My views on marriage don't please you. Do you disagree with them? Would you be content to live like that—in different parts of the world for most of our lives? Would it matter if I wasn't there for anniversaries—for birthdays? What if we had children, and I was away when they were born? If they were ill could you cope alone? God in heaven, Briony!' His tone was derisive. 'You're eighteen years old, and very beautiful. You deserve better prospects for your future happiness than that.'

'Do I?' He was holding her arm, but she dragged herself free. 'How kind of you to make the decision for me, Logan. How very considerate. What I might want for myself is immaterial, of course.'

'No, it's very material.' He was very pale suddenly, and there was a kind of anguish in his eyes. 'It has been since the moment I saw you, God help us both, though I did try to fight it. But you're so young, Briony. How can you be sure what you want?'

'I know I want you,' she said. 'I'm not just out of my depth, Logan. I'm drowning. Are you just going to stand there and let it happen?'

He groaned softly. 'Love—you make things so hard for me. Everything I said that night at the flat still stands. I am too old for you, and not just in age. Do you know what one of my first jobs on a newspaper was—a traffic accident. They were cutting someone out of a car with oxy-acetylene when I got there. He was already dead, and they were in a hurry. Do you know what burning flesh smells like, Briony? I don't think I've ever been so ill in my life. And not only that. There's so much about me that you don't know. All you're really aware of is that you want me to make love to you.'

'Is that so wrong?' she whispered.

'No—on the contrary. But supposing there was something about me—something in my past that you found out about after we were married. Something you couldn't stomach.'

'About you—or about your job?' She was uncertain.

'They're practically indistinguishable.' He took her gently in his arms. 'I'm trying to tell you, Briony, that I hope I'm not the scum of the earth as your father thinks, but God knows I'm no Sir Lancelot either. I've done things I can look back on with a certain amount of pride, and others that I've loathed doing and loathed myself for doing them. That's what the job is. That's what I am. I don't know whether you can take that.'

'I don't know either.' She buried her face in his chest, delighting in the warm smell of him. 'But I can't be happy without you, Logan.'

'You have to be as young as you are to be as certain as that,' he said rather grimly.

'Don't you want to marry me, Logan?' She looked up at him, deliberately veiling her eyes with her long lashes, and allowing the tip of her tongue to penetrate her parted lips.

'I know what I'd like to do to you right now, with or without benefit of clergy.' Logan shook her slightly. 'But not with your aunt's arrival imminent. I suppose she'll give us her blessing. And we'll be married when your father gets home from America.'

Briony quivered slightly. 'Couldn't we be married now, Logan? Right away?'

'No.' His tone was very positive. 'We see your father and we tell him first. He isn't going to be pleased anyway, but he'd be even angrier if he came home and found you married already.'

In the event, Briony could not imagine her father being capable of any more anger, no matter what she had done. He was beside himself with rage, calling her every kind of a fool.

'He's not fit to associate with you, let alone marry you,' he stormed. 'I suppose he sees marriage to the Chairman's daughter as the easy way to an editor's job in the company. Well, he'll soon realise his mistake!'

'Logan isn't interested in the editorial side of the newspaper production,' Briony said wearily. It was a point they had discussed together quite extensively. 'Daddy, I know he wouldn't be your choice for me in a million years, but can't you be happy for me because I'm happy?'

'Happiness?' Sir Charles gave a bark of disbelieving laughter. 'A man like that is incapable of making any woman happy. He probably has women all over the world—and you'll be the legal wife in England. Well, don't imagine for one instant that I'll lend my countenance to the marriage.'

There were inevitably newspaper stories when the news that Logan and Briony planned to wed leaked out and before long the U.P.G.'s rivals were talking openly of the rift between Charles Trevor and his daughter. Sir Charles refused to give any interviews or make any comment, and Briony followed his example rigidly. The days before the wedding were like some terrible ordeal, especially as Logan was in Paris covering a trade conference and was not expected back until the day before the ceremony.

Aunt Hes, who had offered the cottage in Yorkshire as a honeymoon retreat, was sympathetic to Briony's plight, but already becoming preoccupied with her new book.

Briony began to wonder if anyone really wished them well for the future. Under the congratulations and good wishes at the office, she thought she detected a polite scepticism about their chances of happiness, which bewildered her.

She was alone in the cuttings library at U.P.G. on her final day at work when Karen Wellesley came in. Briony glanced up, astonished, because it was unlike the women's editor to perform a menial task like fetching any cuttings she might need herself.

Karen walked over and stood looking down at her, and with a sinking heart Briony realised that this was the confrontation that she had dreaded.

'So Logan has decided to opt for the boss's daughter,' Karen began, her tone strident. 'How did you manage to trap him into it, dear? Let him get you pregnant?' Her contemptuous glance skimmed Briony's slim figure, resting pointedly on her abdomen.' I hope your father decides to let bygones be bygones eventually, or it will all have been for nothing.'

Briony kept her voice steady. 'I suppose you know what you're talking about, Miss Wellesley.'

'Don't play the innocent with me, darling, because it

doesn't wash. You wanted Logan from the moment you set eyes on him, and you went after him.' Karen's voice was ugly. 'Well, now you've got him—but let's see if you can keep him. I hope you didn't promise him too many crumbs from Daddy's table, because something tells me that you aren't going to be able to deliver. Hard lines, Miss Trevor. You'll find Logan doesn't appreciate being made a fool of any more than your father does. In fact you've stumbled from the hands of one ruthless man to another. And if I had to vote for which of them was the biggest bastard, I think I'd walk into Logan's lobby. Good luck, sweetie—I think you're going to need it.'

Briony sat sick and shaking after Karen had gone, leaving a strong hint of the strong musky perfume she wore in the air. Karen and Logan had been lovers, although she had tried very hard not to think about that, long before she, Briony, had come on the scene. It could be argued that Karen knew him better than most people. It could also be argued that she still cared about him. Certainly her attitude just now had been that of a jealous rather than an indifferent woman.

Ruthless, Briony thought, she said ruthless. And a bigger bastard than my father. And a long shiver ran down her spine.

Lying in bed, trying to snatch what warmth she could from the rapidly cooling hot water bottle, Briony wondered soberly if Karen's words hadn't provided the first serious crack in her precarious edifice of happiness. Yet it had been here in this very cottage that the whole fragile structure had come tumbling about her ears. Almost convulsively she turned on to her stomach, burying her face in the pillow, willing herself to forget, to get some rest, so that in the morning she could go down, get her car started somehow and drive away from here—anywhere. She might have to spend this night under th same roof with Logan, but she would stay no longer. It was all too painfully reminiscent of the honeymoon which had gone so horribly, painfully wrong.

Yet where could she go where these memories would not pursue her? Lying in the chilly darkness, Briony let herself go on remembering.

CHAPTER FOUR

SHE had been able to bear everything about the wedding—the fact that it had been conducted in a register office and not a church, the battery of press cameras she had to face when she came out with Logan after the ceremony, the fact that her father had kept his vow not to attend, and had not acknowledged her wedding day by so much as a telegram—because she knew that very soon she and Logan would be alone together, heading north for the cottage, and the beginning of their life together.

It was late afternoon when they arrived at the house, a still, hazy day, with clouds drifting low on the fells, and mist rising. She'd been slightly disappointed because she'd wanted to show Logan how beautiful the cottage could be in sunlight, but he'd laughed when she'd confessed as much, pulling her to him and kissing her mouth before he picked her up and lifted her over the threshold in the time-honoured tradition.

'It's beautiful now,' he'd said, and there was a tenderness and a promise mixed with the hunger in his voice. Or had she only imagined it? she wondered drearily.

He'd brought the cases in, checked that the necessary food was in the kitchen, and that the cottage was ready for their occupation while she had stood in the centre of the living room, rigid with sudden shyness, because of the unfamiliarity of it all. She was happy, and she wanted him with all her heart and more, but there was a great step to be taken to bridge that gap between the impossible dream and total reality, and the thought of that step and all that was involved in it made her shake inside. She heard his footsteps coming down the stairs and she tensed all over again—she couldn't help herself, and he came into the room and just stood there, watching her but making no attempt to come close, to take her into his arms as she had half hoped, half feared that he would.

He said quietly, 'There are steaks and the makings of a salad in the kitchen. I'm going off to find champagne somewhere.' He smiled slightly. 'Unless you can think of a more appropriate drink?'

'Hardly.' Her voice sounded young and rather breathless. 'Champagne would be wonderful.'

'It's all going to be wonderful.' His gaze held hers for a moment, and she was tempted to say, 'To hell with champagne. Stay with me, Logan.' But the moment passed and she smiled and nodded brightly.

He said, 'I won't be long.'

Briony heard the cottage door close and saw his tall figure going down the path to the gate. The mist was thickening and he was out of sight before he was even a third of the way down the track. She stood at the window, watching, straining her eyes for a last glimpse of him, as if it was somehow important, then she turned away and went slowly upstairs to start unpacking.

It was good to have something to do, something to think about as she took their clothes out of the cases and laid them side by side in the drawers of the old-fashioned chest in the bedroom. She found her nightgown, white and filmy, and laid it on the bed, but a protracted search refused to reveal any pyjamas for Logan, and she supposed with a feeling of embarrassment that he never bothered with them. It was just another case of the dream clashing with the reality, and the image of Logan as a romantic bridegroom clad in silk waiting chivalrously downstairs while she undressed had never been a valid one, she knew. He had given her this time to herself, to get used to it all, and she should be grateful to him, but when he returned he would expect more than gratitude, much, much more, and she felt both uncertain and inadequate. The air was cool in the bedroom, and she told herself that was why she was shivering a little.

She took a last look round, then headed downstairs to make the salad. She was just going into the living room when she heard someone coming up the path. Logan—back so soon? She could hardly believe it, but she flung open the door to welcome him, and found herself confronted instead by a strange woman.

Aunt Hes hadn't mentioned any newcomers to the village, and something told Briony that this woman wasn't a local, anyway. There was an indefinable air of the city dweller about her. Her clothes were a little too smart, her shoes a little too elaborate for Kirkby Scar.

There was tension in the woman's face, beneath the carefully applied make-up, and the hands were clutching an expensive handbag so tightly that her knuckles showed white.

She said, 'Mrs Adair? Are you Mrs Adair?'

There was doubt in her voice as if she suspected she was the victim of a hoax. It was the first time Briony had been addressed by her married name, and it should have been a great occasion, but somehow it wasn't. She supposed the woman must be a local after all, because no one else knew they had come here. They had carefully let it be known in London that they were going abroad.

Briony said slowly, 'Why, yes. Can I help you—

Mrs...?' She let her voice trail away on a question. If this woman was some sort of welcoming committee, then she had to make her welcome, whatever her private feelings. And for no reason that she could explain, Briony wished with all her heart that this stranger would go away, or that Logan would return, preferably both.

'My name is Chapman—Marina Chapman.' She peered at Briony, and it was an unpleasant sensation. 'You've heard the name, perhaps?'

Briony thought rapidly. 'I don't think so.' She lifted her shoulders apologetically. 'I'm sorry. Should I have done so?'

'Your—husband hasn't mentioned me?'

'No.' Briony was trying to be polite, but her bewilderment was deepening. So this Mrs Chapman wasn't a local busybody come to report on the newly weds, or she would have said she was a friend of Aunt Hes's.

'No, probably not.' Mrs Chapman's lips twisted. 'May I come in?'

Briony wanted to refuse. She had the strangest impulse to slam the door and close this woman out, but good manners insisted she should stand aside and let her walk past her into the house. She opened the parlour door and ushered her in. The room felt close and still, and slightly chilly. A fly was buzzing at the window and she went across to release it and admit some air, but dank mist swirled in, and she closed the casement again hastily.

She turned to face Mrs Chapman. 'We've only just arrived, but I think there's some coffee in the kitchen, or tea if you prefer. My husband isn't here just now. He's gone to fetch some—things that we forgot. I hope he won't be long because the weather's getting worse all the time. I'd forgotten how quickly the mist could come down. Did you bring a car?'

She was aware that she was babbling, and that Mrs

Chapman was standing just inside the parlour door, watching her steadily, her expression almost inimical. Anger came to Briony's rescue. She said with sudden heat, 'Look here, Mrs Chapman. I'd be glad if you could tell me what you want and then go. We are on our honeymoon.'

'I'm quite aware of that, Mrs Adair. And I know your husband isn't here because I watched him leave. I wanted to see you alone, you see. I wanted to tell you the kind of man you'd married.'

Briony said, 'You'd better go.' She had some wild idea that Mrs Chapman might be one of Logan's discarded mistresses, but she was obviously much older than him and not a type that Briony thought would have had much appeal for him. She moved forward, but Mrs Chapman was standing her ground between Briony and the door. She was fumbling in her bag now, producing papers, newspaper cuttings, Briony saw.

'Not until you've seen these.' She threw them down on the table in the centre of the room, spilling them across its polished surface. Briony looked down at them, puzzled, her attention caught in spite of herself. She began to read the ones on top. They seemed to concern an inquest on someone who had committed suicide, she realised. There was a picture of a man, probably the deceased, and other pictures too, some of a woman. This woman.

'My husband,' Mrs Chapman said flatly. 'He killed himself.'

'I'm very sorry,' said Briony. She felt wholly inadequate in the face of the grief and rage she seemed to feel emanating from this woman. She was like one of the Furies from an ancient Greek tragedy, a figure of vengeance, only the Furies had also been known as the Kindly Ones, and there was nothing kind about Marina Chapman as she stood there, her eyes fixed relentlessly on Briony's face.

'He shot himself,' Mrs Chapman went on after a pause. 'And your husband drove him to it.'

'Oh, no!' Briony said quickly. 'You're wrong. You must be wrong. I——'

'He drove him to it,' Mrs Chapman repeated relentlessly. 'With his prying, and his endless, endless bloody questions. Harry got desperate. He had the answers, all the answers, but your husband never gave him time to think, time to answer. He was always phoning, or on the doorstep. And every day these stories in the paper—just the one he worked for at first, and then all the others. Then they all came gathering like vultures, asking questions, printing their vile lies—lies your husband told them about Harry. Then the police. Harry was a good man—a good man!' Her voice became high-pitched with her insistence. 'He didn't do these things. He hadn't defrauded anyone. He could have explained everything. But your husband never gave him a chance. He dragged his name in the mud, and still he wasn't content. Always questions. No bloody peace—ever!'

Briony put her hands over her ears. 'I don't want to hear any more!'

'My Harry didn't want to hear any more,' Mrs Chapman said. 'But your husband made him. And he was only the first—the chief jackal, the leader of the pack. Filthy scavengers the lot of them, nosing through dirt!'

Her tone was hysterical, and Briony was afraid suddenly. The woman sounded almost unhinged, and they were alone in the house.

She said, 'Mrs Chapman, won't you sit down, and let me get you something—a cup of coffee. Then we'll talk about this. You say your husband was a good man—well, I feel the same about my husband and . . .'

'But you don't know him, do you?' said Mrs Chapman. 'You've only known him a few weeks. It was in all the papers—a whirlwind romance, they called it. And you've only been married a matter of hours. What do you know about him? Only what you want to know. That he's an attractive man—oh, I'll grant you that—that he makes you feel good in bed?' She saw the sudden flare of colour in Briony's pale cheeks and laughed harshly. 'God, don't you even know that yet? What an innocent! No wonder ...' She stopped.

'No wonder what?' Briony asked numbly.

'It doesn't matter.' The older woman's voice was dismissive. 'All that matters is that you should know the type of man you've married. Someone who's hunted down an innocent man—made his life a hell on earth. Someone who'd sell his own mother—or you—for a good story with his name on it. Do you know that everything he wrote about poor Harry—every lie, every vile insinuation had his name blazoned on it—as if he was proud of it.'

Briony heard herself say, 'You must be wrong. There must be some mistake.'

'There's no mistake. Your husband murdered mine as surely as if he'd taken the gun in his own hand and pulled the trigger. And how many other lives has he destroyed—this "ace investigative reporter"?' She spat the words as if they were slime. 'Who else has he trampled over to make his headlines—to get himself noticed—to make his way to the top? Who else has been hounded and persecuted until he couldn't take any more?' She broke off, her voice suddenly choked with sobs.

Briony turned away. There was something vaguely indecent in this grief following on the heels of near-violence, and she felt nauseated. Almost inconsequentially, she noticed that the mist had thickened still more, and it was now hardly possible to see more than a few yards from the window.

Behind her, Mrs Chapman stirred. She was clearly trying to regain her tenuous hold on her composure.

She said, 'I'll go now, Mrs Adair. I'll leave the cuttings. They're only duplicates. I have a full file at home. But I felt you had a right to know, and that it was my duty to warn you if no one else would. I wish you well, believe it or not, and I hope that you find—love is enough, because you'll never be able to trust him.'

Briony, standing motionless by the window, heard the front door close. She saw Mrs Chapman, her head slightly bent, walk down the path towards the gate, then the mist swallowed her up.

Briony began to shake. She turned and gathered up the scattered cuttings, intending to take them into the living room and put them on the fire, but almost in spite of herself began to examine them, turning them over. From each one Logan's name seemed to scream out at her in bold black type, even on the report of Harry Chapman's death. Found in the study of his house, the report ran, with head wounds. Briony shuddered, pressing her balled fist against her mouth. Who had found him? she wondered. Marina Chapman? A housekeeper? She had seen a picture of the house they lived in. It was the sort of sprawling neo-Tudor mansion which made some sort of living-in help essential.

She went slowly through the cuttings until she found the report of the inquest. There were in fact several of them culled from different newspapers, some rather sensational in treatment. One of them reported in detail some remarks made by the coroner while a verdict of suicide was being returned. Phrases like 'respected member of the business community'—'intolerable pressures'—'unwarranted persecutions by the less responsible sections of the Press'—'gutter journalism'—'terrible tragedy' seemed to leap out at her, burning at her brain, as she tried to assimilate them. They were repeated to a greater or lesser extent in the other cuttings. The coroner's words had obviously made a strong impression on those present, as they had been intended to. She read them again, more slowly. There was only one way that they could be interpreted—as an attack on Logan and the campaign he had mounted against the dead man. She began to search through the cuttings for a date, and found one at last. This must have been about the last story Logan had worked on before he joined the *Courier*, she realised, and began to feel sick. Had this story been his passport to Fleet Street and a top job on a top newspaper? Was this what Marina Chapman had been getting at? And slowly and reluctantly, she began to remember all the things her father had said in the past as well.

She had no idea how long she stood there motionless by the table, the cuttings still clutched in her hands, her mind whirling on a terrified treadmill of revulsion and rejection, but when at last she came to herself with a slight start she was chilled to the bone, and wondering what had recalled her. Some distant noise—the slam of a car door perhaps—indicating that Logan had returned.

She gave a little choking cry and flung the cuttings down on the ground before she turned and ran out of the room. Her sheepskin coat was lying across a chair in the living room and she snatched it up on her way towards the kitchen. The bolt was still undrawn on the back door and it resisted her first efforts. She struggled with it, fright warring with frustration within her. She was conscious only of the need for flight—the knowledge that she couldn't face Logan or the demands he was now legally entitled to make of her, feeling as she did. She didn't even flinch as the bolt suddenly gave way, scraping her finger painfully and drawing blood. She felt as if she was bleeding to death inside as it was.

The mist closed around her as she dived through the back door, thrusting her arms through the sleeves of her coat and dragging its warmth around her. She ran past the overgrown vegetable garden, and the ancient shed, and ducked beneath a sagging wire fence on to the open fellside.

She knew her way to the huddle of stones at the top of the fell almost by instinct. She had spent a number of holidays at the cottage with Aunt Hes in the past, and a climb to the top of the fell had always been part of it—like a pilgrimage. She'd intended to make Logan walk up there with her. Apart from the fantastic view, it had always been a special place for her, and she wanted to share it with him. Now she was frantically glad that he would not know where she had gone in the mist or where to follow, thankful that she had a refuge where she could hide until she could think clearly and decide what she must do.

She was breathless and gasping when she reached the top, with a painful stitch in her side. She leaned against one of the rocks for support, pressing her hand against her body, until the worst of the pain was past. Then she sank down on her haunches, her back against the rock, and began to steady her ragged breathing. There was quite a wind blowing, and the mist was patchier here on top of the fell. Briony huddled further into her coat.

She dropped her head into her hands and tried to think, but words and phrases she had read in the cuttings kept intruding. There had been a photograph too of Marina and Harry Chapman on their wedding day, and a shudder went through her as the full irony of that came home to her.

She told herself 'It can't be true. Logan wouldn't do

that. The Coroner must have meant someone else.' But even to her own ears, it sounded pitiful, and totally lacking in assurance.

For the fact was that she knew very little of what Logan might or might not be capable of doing. She remembered some of the things he himself had told her, and how they had sickened him, but he had filed his copy just the same. He hadn't packed journalism in with disgust and chosen a less fraught existence. And what about all the things he hadn't told her—of which the Harry Chapman episode might only be one?

She had first met him after all at the awards party, and he'd been given the 'Journalist of the Year' title. He'd claimed it meant nothing, but she knew that no one was even considered for such an award for merely covering flower shows and Women's Institute meetings. Before she had ever laid eyes on him, she had read his work, and known it to be tough and hard-hitting.

She had heard her father on the power of the Press so many times, she had come to regard it as a secret joke, but it had never occurred to her that the power might be such that it might drive a man to lift a loaded gun to his head and pull the trigger. That, Briony thought, was an abuse of power. And she could not even make the excuse that Logan had been made to write what he did. He could have refused as a matter of principle.

But he hadn't refused, and the fact remained that Harry Chapman was dead—suicide while the balance of his mind was disturbed. And she was married to the man who had disturbed that balance. The pressure on Harry Chapman had come from Logan. And from others. But what had Marina Chapman called him? 'The leader of the pack'.

At the small reception which Aunt Hes had given for them at her flat, Hal Mackenzie had been unusually ebullient, his arm round Logan's shoulders and hers. 'Look after him, sweetheart, because he's the best. Where he leads, the others follow.'

At the time she'd felt a swift glow of pride, in no way dispelled by Logan's mocking and self-denigrating retort, but now she felt cold and empty at the memory. She'd seen a television film once about wild dogs, and how they hunted down their prey in packs, concentrating on the weakest quarry, the one most likely to break under pressure.

She shivered, crouching under her sheltering rock, then tensed slightly, peering downwards through the swirl of the mist. A glimmer of light had appeared, and she knew what it was: Logan had returned to the cottage and had put the lights on. Probably he was going from room to room, looking for her, maybe believing that she was hiding from him to tease him. She wondered how soon he would find the scattered cuttings on the parlour floor and realise the truth, and what he would do when the realisation did dawn.

It was dark now, and the chill and the damp were really getting to her, and there was a darkness inside her too, while below her the light in the cottage stared up like an accusing eye. But why should I feel accused? she thought. I'm not the guilty one. And she heard ringing in her ears Marina Chapman's harsh gibe, 'What an innocent!' She put her hands to her face and began to cry, harsh choking sobs which tore at her throat and chest. She sank further down on to the ground, uncaring about the icy dampness which seemed to seep into her bones. The unyielding earth was a comfort and a support, and the most she could hope for in a world that seemed to offer no hope at all.

She supposed that she must have cried herself to sleep, because the next thing she remembered was a confusion of voices and torches and a dog thrusting its wet nose into her hand. Dazedly she looked up into a face that was vaguely familiar. After a moment she realised it was the farmer whose land bordered the cottage.

'Now then, lass, what's to do?' His voice was genial enough, but she sensed a puzzled note as well. 'Could you not find your way down again?'

'Oh, Mr Masters!' Briony scrambled to her feet, aware of her wan, bedraggled appearance. 'I—I'm sorry. Have you been looking for me?' She glanced round the small group confronting her, recognising two of the men who worked on the farm, and another whose identity she was not aware of.

'It weren't much of a search,' Mr Masters assured her. 'Just as well.' He gave a slight guffaw. 'You've left that man of yours in a right state. Wanted to come with us, he did, but I told him he was best to stay where he was and get the bed warm for you.' He guffawed again, and the men with him joined in. Briony felt her cheeks flaming.

'Get lost, did you?' Mr Masters sent her a narrow look as they began to make their way down the fellside. Briony noticed that the mist had pretty well cleared, and that the sky above was speckled with stars. 'Daft sort of weather for walking in. What were you thinking of?'

Briony forced a smile. 'I just—felt like some air,' she answered stiltedly. 'I—I didn't realise the mist was so bad.'

Mr Masters shrugged as if her behaviour was beyond him. 'Happen you took a nasty chance,' he observed unanswerably.

It was almost like being taken back in custody, she thought hysterically, as they approached the cottage. Logan was waiting at the back door, and his expression was not encouraging. Briony went past him, not meeting his gaze, and walked through into the living room, crouching down on the rug and stretching her freezing hands out to the flickering flames in the hearth. She could hear Logan talking to the men in the kitchen, but their voices were pitched too low for her to catch the words. She guessed Logan was thanking them, and presently she heard a burst of rather ribald laughter and a chorus of goodnights. Then the back door slammed.

She waited, unable to move, every nerve in her body stretched to screaming point.

Eventually Logan came into the room. He moved as if he was intensely weary and his expression was unreadable. He was carrying a tray which held a steaming bowl, some bread and a spoon.

'Soup,' he said briefly, setting the tray down on the table.

'Logan——' she began apprehensively, sitting back on her heels.

'Eat first.' His voice and eyes were implacable as he gestured her towards the table. 'The time for talking comes later.'

The soup was out of a tin, but it warmed her all the way down to her toes, even though afterwards she could not remember what flavour it had been. She had to force the last few spoonfuls past the tight knot of nervousness in her throat. It seemed terribly important for some reason that she should finish every drop.

'Thank you,' she said when she had finished. 'That was—delicious.'

'Although far from what I had in mind,' he returned with equal courtesy. 'But then very little has been, so far.' He got up from his chair and came towards her, and she could not prevent herself from flinching away from him.

He paused and smiled grimly. 'Don't look so scared, Briony. I'm not going to touch you. I wouldn't trust myself for one thing, and for another, I wouldn't want to drive you into a second flight on our wedding night. I'm sure our neighbours are already wondering what sadistic perversions I've been threatening you with to drive you out on to the fells for refuge. A reputation as a Bluebeard or worse isn't quite what I'd bargained for on our honeymoon, I must confess.'

'But it wasn't like that,' she began quickly.

'Wasn't it? Then suppose you tell me how it was?' She could feel the anger which blazed in him, though he had it well under control. 'Or can the explanation be found in that pile of garbage in the other room?'

'You found the cuttings,' she said in a low voice.

'Wasn't I intended to? What I'd like to know is how they got there.'

'She brought them—Mrs Chapman.'

'Marina Chapman?' His tone conveyed total incredulity. 'You're trying to tell me that she's come out of tax exile in Jersey and travelled all the way to Yorkshire to deliver a pile of yellowing history to you? Oh, come off it, Briony!'

'It's the truth.' Briony made a helpless gesture. 'She—just arrived. I didn't know who she was until she introduced herself. But I would have recognised her from her photographs anyway.'

'I don't doubt that,' he said tautly. 'Marina always had the gift of looking after herself, physically and in every other way. But what did she say to you that could make you run off like that? My God, you could have died of pneumonia—or exposure—up there!'

'But I didn't die, I'm very much alive. It's her husband, Harry Chapman, who's dead. That's what she came to tell me about, Logan. She came to tell me about her husband and how he died, and the part you played in it.'

'The part—I played?' His brows rose as he stared down at her, and she saw his jaw tighten. 'I'm beginning to see. You read the inquest reports, did you? Absorbed the coroner's remarks about the gutter press and innocent men?' He swore viciously. 'There wasn't a soul in that courtroom, the coroner included, who didn't know that the whole investigation we'd mounted into Chapman's affairs had gone to the Director of Public Prosecutions. His arrest was imminent, and his conviction was a certainty, so he shot himself.'

'But his wife said he was innocent,' she argued. 'She said he'd never defrauded anyone and ...'

'I suppose he can be acquitted of that, technically at least. But innocent?' Logan shook his head. 'Let me tell you about Chapman, my sweet. He was a small-time builder with delusions of grandeur when he began. When he died, he was a wealthy man owning a number of companies and with a controlling interest in others. There were samples of his—handiwork as a builder all over the surrounding counties, and he was preparing to go country-wide. He had to be stopped.'

'Because he was a bad builder?' she asked bitterly.

'Because he was totally corrupt.' She had never heard such contempt in anyone's voice. 'Chapman would never have been awarded a contract to build an outside privy if he'd simply tendered in open competition, so he devised his own method. He started in a small way by passing graft to a few poorly paid officials on local councils, and gradually worked his way up until he'd bought chairmen of Planning committees, County surveyors—the lot.' His mouth was hard. 'I saw some of the monstrosities he put up. An old people's home where the foundations hadn't been properly laid—flats where you could get two fingers in the gaps round the window frames, houses where the bedrooms were so damp that there was actually fungus growing on the walls. No one could understand why he got so many contracts when people were saying openly he was nothing better than a jerry-builder, so my editor who happened to have the novel theory that human beings deserve decent places to live in decided to take a closer interest in his activities. We turned over a few stones, and all kinds of interesting things came squirming out into the light of day. Eventually, someone who'd been on the take from Chapman and was now scared stiff of the consequences decided to talk to us—and to the police, incidentally, but that came later. But Chapman had taken his precautions. He'd salted away the money in his wife's name—oh, his grieving widow knew exactly what he'd been up to all along—and bought her a tax haven in Jersey. All he had to do was stand trial and serve his sentence, along with all the other poor devils he'd drawn into his net, but he didn't have the guts for that.'

His voice sank almost to a whisper. 'So will you please tell me now what there is in the Harry Chapman story to make you run away from me—because that's what you did, wasn't it, Briony—even if not for the salacious reasons that your gallant rescue party have no doubt dreamed up by now?'

'She said you'd murdered him. She said you were a jackal—that you'd printed lies about him—that he was an innocent man.'

'And you were so ready to believe her that you couldn't even wait to ask if it was true.' He laughed softly, and the sound of it seemed to flay her skin like a whip. 'First rule of journalism, sweet wife—always get a quote from the other side before you print, even if it's "no comment." '

She wrapped her arms round her midriff in an unconscious gesture of defence.

'Logan, I'm sorry ...'

'Sorry?' he interrupted violently. 'You're supposed to be in love with me—for better for worse, the whole bit, remember? Yet we've only been married a couple of hours when you run out on me on the say-so of a complete stranger—and then you have the nerve to say you're sorry!'

'I don't know what you expect me to say.' All the colour had drained from her face during his tirade.

'Exactly what you did say, I suppose. I'd forgotten that you're your father's daughter, Briony. Daddy's brainwashing has really worked, hasn't it? Gutter press—jackal—persecutor of the innocent. That's why you were so ready to lap up Marina Chapman's farrago of nonsense—because you half-believed it already. Because in spite of anything you may have said in the past, you really haven't the slightest faith in my integrity at all.'

She closed her eyes. She did not dare to speak—to defend herself against what she knew was the truth of his allegations. She could have defended him, and shown Marina Chapman the door, but she had not done so. She had stayed and listened and wondered, then believed and run away.

He said flatly, 'I told you that there'd been things in my life that I hadn't enjoyed doing. And I wondered if you could accept that. Well, now we both know the answer to that, don't we?'

'I really am sorry.' She hardly dared lift her eyes to his face. 'It was just such a shock—her arriving like that, and the things she said.'

'Oh, the timing was perfect, I grant you.' His mouth twisted satirically. 'The only thing she couldn't gauge was your reaction, and even that worked out just right.'

He gave a mirthless laugh. 'Good for Marina! She's waited a long time for her revenge, and travelled a long way for it. Your co-operation must have delighted her.'

Briony said, 'What do you want me to say? What do you want me to do?'

'I think you've said and done enough.' He gave her a level glance. 'We'll decide in the morning what to do. In the meantime, you'd better get some rest—you look completely bushed.' He saw the startled expression on her face, the widening of her eyes, and lifted his brows interrogatively. 'What's the matter.'

'What must I do—grovel?' she demanded defiantly, a flicker of resentment beginning to burn at his cool dismissal of her.

His aquamarine eyes assumed an enigmatic expression. 'Perhaps. Anyway, we'll talk in the morning. Goodnight, Briony.'

Briony gasped. Her first assumption was quite correct. Logan was just—dismissing her, and in a particularly humiliating manner. The undoubted implication in his words was that she was to go to bed alone, and that he had no intention of joining her later.

Her voice quivered a little as she said, 'I don't feel like going to bed. I think we should talk now. I—I made an error of judgment, and I'm sorry. I've admitted as much. But you're treating me as if I'm guilty of some crime, and I won't have it.'

'I think that to dash off into the mist and stay away for hours because you've suddenly decided that your husband is a murderer ranks as slightly more than an error of judgment,' Logan said grimly. 'However, go on, Briony. Apparently it's your turn to feel aggrieved, so let's have the whole thing out in the open.'

She looked down at her clasped hands. 'This is—supposed to be our wedding night,' she began.

'The significance of the occasion hasn't been exactly lost on me—nor on a number of people, I suspect. Please continue.'

She shrugged helplessly. 'You know what I'm trying to say.'

'I think so. You've deduced from my remarks that I have no intention of sleeping with you tonight. Well, your deduction is correct.'

'But why?'

'My God, Briony!' He gave her a weary look. 'Do I really have to spell it out to you? Let's just say that the events of the last few hours have—cooled my ardour where you are concerned. Marriage isn't just going to bed—it's the building of a relationship which has to be founded on trust, and that's what I was fool enough to believe we could do. Hellfire, if I'd wanted just to take you to bed, I could have done so weeks ago, and without marriage. Did it never occur to you to ask why I didn't take what you were so patently ready to give me?'

Her cheeks were burning, and she did not know where to look. 'No,' she said chokingly. 'But I'm sure you're going to tell me.'

'Let me remind you, sweetheart, that you wanted this confrontation, not me,' he gritted. 'I left you untouched because I didn't want to take advantage of you, or rush you into something that you weren't ready for. Oh, I don't mean physically. You have a beautiful, nubile body, and nothing would stop me wanting you. But I felt that you were unready mentally and emotionally, and God knows you've proved me right. It seems to me that to try and carry on with a conventional honeymoon in the circumstances would be a farce. Besides, although I've tried hard to control it, I'm bloody angry with you, and I don't want to take you in anger.'

'Fleet Street's answer to Sir Galahad. Is that your new image? You—hypocrite!'

The darkening of his face should have been warning enough, but she went recklessly on. 'It's a side to your nature the Chapmans wouldn't recognise—or Hal Mackenzie for that matter. You're a man who knows how to put the pressure on and keep it there—remember? All right, so I was shocked to hear the lengths you were prepared to go to maintain that pressure, but I think that's a fairly normal reaction under the circumstances, and I refuse to be treated like some idiot child bride just because ...'

The words faltered and ran dry as she read his face.

'So how do you want to be treated?' He asked the question quite softly, but there was a note in his voice which made her blood run cold. 'Like a bride, but not a child—is that it? Well, I'll accommodate you, sweetheart'—he made the endearment sound like an obscenity—'in fact I promise you'll leave childhood behind you for ever. But just remember that you asked for it.'

He came towards her, and she realised too late just what she had invited by her display of petulance. She jumped up and tried to dash past him towards the kitchen, but he caught her quite easily by the arm, his fingers bruising her flesh as he dragged her towards him.

'You're running nowhere else tonight, my dear wife,' he said almost dispassionately.

'Logan, please don't!' She beat at his chest with clenched fists as his arms closed round her. 'I didn't mean ...'

'Oh, you meant it,' he said. 'Just as I mean this.'

His mouth was savage on hers, bruising the softness of her lips, making her taste the salt of her own blood. She moaned a little, twisting her head, trying to escape the harsh pressure, but his hands came up, twisting into her hair, forcing her brutally to stand still and submit to his demands. When he released her her legs were shaking so much she felt as if she was going to collapse, and her protest was barely audible as he swung her up into his arms and started towards the door with her.

They were climbing the stairs now, and she began to struggle in his arms, her sense of panic overwhelming her. 'Please—Logan!'

He snarled in reply, turning her head towards him so that her face was muffled in the thin dark wool of the sweater he was wearing. She couldn't see, she could hardly breathe, but with every nerve in her body she was aware of the darkness in him, the violence.

After the shadows of the staircase the bedroom seemed suddenly glaringly light, and agonisingly small. Briony stood in the middle of it, feeling like a trapped animal, watching Logan lock the door and put the key in his pocket.

'There's the bed you're so anxious to share with me, my sweet.' There was no softening in his face as he looked at her. He was a stranger, implacable and terrifying. 'And you won't need this.' He picked up the nightdress she had laid on it a lifetime before and tore it from bodice to hem, before dropping it on the floor behind him. 'Now take your clothes off,' he said almost gently. 'Unless you want the same thing to happen to them.'

Her mouth was dry and her hands clumsy as she obeyed him. She found she was folding each article of clothing neatly as she removed it, and placing it on the waiting chair as if she was still a child at boarding school. It was a habit she hadn't indulged in for a long while, and she knew she was only playing for time. But Logan showed no sign of impatience, or even that he was aware of her delaying tactics. He watched her in silence, his face cynical and even slightly bored, as if he was witnessing a third-rate striptease performance. He made no move to help her or touch her in any way, and when at last she stood there, trying to shield herself with her arms, she suddenly remembered the evening he had begun to make love to her at his flat—his kisses, the gentleness of his hands—and a hard knot of misery welled up inside her.

'Tears already!' He gave a soft laugh. 'And I've hardly started on you yet. I'm the man who knows how to put the pressure on and keep it there—remember? Your own words, darling.' He peeled off his sweater and threw it on the bed, then began to unbuckle the belt of his pants. 'And I intend to make you regret every last syllable.'

'I regret them now.' She moistened her lips desperately. 'Logan, for God's sake! You'll make us hate each other ...'

'The word is love,' he said. 'We make love, not hate. You'll be surprised to discover how closely one can resemble the other. Or you will be by morning. Don't stand there shivering, darling. Get into bed.'

She did as she was told, closing her eyes, and pulling the sheet up to her chin. Presently the light went out and there was a faint protesting creak from the mattress as Logan lowered his weight on to the bed beside her. She lay there rigid with tension, waiting for him to touch her, dreading the resumption of the brutality he had inflicted on her downstairs.

He said, 'You can start breathing again, Briony. I don't intend to rape you. I never did. Downstairs you asked me if I wanted you to grovel. Well, I think I do and I think you will. But you won't be begging for mercy. On the contrary, you'll be pleading with me to put you out of your misery.'

He touched her then, his fingers cupping the softness of one breast, caressing, teasing, arousing. She felt a shock of desire go through her, and heard him laugh again.

'You're going to pay a high price for your initiation into womanhood, my sweet,' his voice taunted her from the darkness. 'I hope you'll think it's worth it.'

Lying alone in the cold, silent room, she remembered. She remembered everything. At first she had been angry, and determined that his cynical expectations would not be fulfilled. Closing her mind against him had been relatively simple, but there was no guard, no restraint she could place upon her slowly awakening senses. Quite gently at first, then with growing insistence, Logan used his hands and mouth to bring every inch of her body to quivering vibrant life. One by one, she surrendered her pitiful defences to his expertise as a lover, and waited for the moment of consummation.

But it did not arrive, and slowly, gradually realisation began to dawn that this was exactly what he intended. She was to be reduced—or exalted—to a state of wordless, mindless passion, and then abandoned there in a kind of sensual limbo from which only he could provide her release. And that he had no intention of releasing her, he soon made clear.

She was clinging to him, her fingers stretched over the smooth muscularity of his back as he leaned over her, her lips parted as she moaned his name, willing him to kiss her mouth, to hold her, to come into her.

Her eyes had grown accustomed to the darkness and she could see his face quite plainly as he bent towards her, the aquamarine eyes studying her with a curious intentness, his mouth twisting suddenly in a small cruel smile.

He said softly, 'Have I made you want me, Briony? Now, make me want you.'

Then he was moving, not towards her but away, turning his back on her. She lay beside him, dizzy and feverish with the desire he had roused in her, stunned by a rejection she could barely comprehend. She wanted to hit out, to scream, to weep with torment and frustration, but instead she made herself lie very still beside him, gazing with burning eyes into the shadows of the room until the soft regularity of his breathing told her that he had fallen asleep. Then and only then did she relax her rigidity and allow herself the luxury of tears.

She cried in silence, her throat and chest convulsed in pain, her fist pressed to her mouth to prevent one whimper escaping. Slowly, as she cried, the deep ache in her body began to subside, and eventually she fell into a shallow, restless doze.

Almost before she had opened her unwilling eyes to face a grey dawn, she had known that she was alone in the bed. She raised herself up wearily on one elbow and stared round the room, registering that Logan's clothes had gone. She threw back the covers and got out, shivering as the morning chill struck at her naked body, and reached for her own things.

As she walked towards the door she felt something tangle round her foot. She glanced down and saw it was her torn nightdress. With a grimace, she bent and picked it up. This was one garment she never wanted to see again as long as she lived, she thought, and she could make sure that she never did.

Her footsteps sounded very loud on the stairs, but they echoed emptily, as if the house was deserted. It took all her courage to open the living room door and go in, but there was no one there. The ashes were grey, but still warm in the fireplace, and after a moment's hesitation she screwed her nightdress into a ball and dropped it on top of them before setting a lighted match to it. It flared up briefly and was gone.

Very symbolic, Briony thought almost dispassionately.

Her soup bowl, she noticed, had vanished from the table, and she found it washed and on the draining rack in the kitchen. There was evidence that Logan had made himself coffee and toast before he had departed—where? The back door was unbolted, and the kettle was still warm, which seemed to suggest he had not gone far. As she began to refill the kettle for her own coffee, she saw him coming the way she had come down from the fell the previous night. She made herself stay in the kitchen and go on with the paraphernalia of coffee brewing as if unaware of his approach, but she was forced to acknowledge his presence as he unlatched the back door and came in.

She turned slightly and saw him standing in the doorway watching her, his head thrown back slightly. He looked arrogant and forbidding, and his brows were drawn together frowningly.

'Good morning,' Briony said quietly.

'A conventional opening if not a truthful one.' He came into the kitchen kicking the door shut behind him.

She shrugged, even managed a smile. 'I thought I'd play safe for once. Do you want some coffee?'

'No, thank you,' he said. 'I had some earlier, before I went walking. Now I want to talk.'

'I don't think there's anything to talk about.' She added hot water to the coffee granules as if her life depended on getting the formula just right. 'You made your point more than adequately last night. I should have been more grateful, but as you'll appreciate, I wasn't seeing things too clearly just then. Now, everything is perfectly simple. We can go back to London and live our separate lives, and I'll apply for an annulment. It will be quicker than a divorce. I think you have to wait two years for that.'

There was a long, still silence after she had finished

speaking. She put milk and sugar into her coffee and stirred it with minute attention.

'That was an interesting little speech,' Logan said slowly. 'Have you been rehearsing it for long?'

'I haven't been rehearsing it at all,' she said. 'But I think it sums up the situation pretty well.'

'It sums up nothing.' He came and stood behind her, close but not quite touching, so that she could feel the warmth of his breath on her neck. His voice sounded different, softer but more urgent. He said, 'It's cold in this kitchen. Come where it's warmer and talk to me. Better still, come back to bed with me. I'll make you forget last night ever happened.'

She said, and her voice was like ice, 'You'll make me forget nothing, Logan, do you hear. And please don't come any closer or put your hands on me. I'd rather die than have you touch me again.'

The web of tension spun around them, closing them in. Briony closed her eyes awaiting the explosion, the inevitable outburst. She gripped the edge of the formica work surface until it cut painfully into her hand. She sensed rather than felt Logan's withdrawal, and her relief was so overwhelming that her legs nearly gave way under her.

His voice was cold and sardonic as he said, 'Stay alive, Briony, stay alive. I don't want you on my conscience as well.'

Then he turned away, and she heard him cross the living room and go out, closing the door behind him.

CHAPTER FIVE

BRIONY sat up in bed, pushing her tumbled hair out of her eyes. It did not do any good to relive these painful memories, she told herself angrily. All it did was demonstrate the importance that they still assumed in her life—a fruitless reminder if ever there was one.

Suddenly restless, she flung back the covers and got out of bed, padding over to the window and jerking back the curtain. The room was full of icy draughts and she shivered uncontrollably as she stared out into the darkness. The air was whirling with white flakes, and the landscape outside was totally alien under its muffling blanket of snow. She fought a rising sense of panic as she realised that this was not an isolated snowstorm to be followed by a rapid thaw, but that winter had caught her here under the same roof with Logan, and seemed intent on keeping her here. Her hopes of a speedy and discreet exit as soon as daylight dawned were fading rapidly.

But I can't stay here, she thought wildly. I should have got out earlier, while the going was good. The snow wasn't nearly as deep then. It couldn't have been. Logan got here; I could have left—I should have left. Now it's too late. Too late. The words seemed to reverberate inside her head, and she lifted a shaking hand to her temple before turning away from the window with a last defeated look at the blizzard raging on the other side of the glass.

She got reluctantly back into bed and lay down, trying to compose herself for sleep, but it was an almost impossible task. The memories she had revived were too raw to be easily put aside.

She tossed and turned, punching her pillow into shape, witching at the bedclothes, trying to deny the truth which was beginning to force itself upon her all too conscious mind. Reliving the miseries of her wedding night had not been total grief. They had aroused her too.

It was not altogether surprising, she tried to excuse herself. After all, it was in this very bed that Logan had kissed and caressed her to the point of no return, to the point of madness, and then turned from her. For a few dark, dangerous moments it would have been fatally easy o imagine that he had actually been beside her, his mouth warm and sensuous on her breasts, his exploring hands a pleasurable torment.

She sank her teeth into her lower lip, trying to force he image of him out of her mind, loathing herself for her body's betrayal, as she had loathed herself in that grey dawn months before.

Her sole comfort was that at least Logan did not know hat she was lying here wanting him.

Oh God, she had admitted it at last. She wanted him, nd she had never stopped wanting him, in spite of the hings that humiliation and the fear of another rejection had made her say.

She'd wanted him on that bleak dreadful drive later in he day back to London. He'd driven too fast, fiddling all he time with the radio, turning from channel to channel n search of music until she'd felt like screaming. But it had been important not to scream, she remembered. It had been important to lean back in her seat calm and uncaring on the surface, and pray that in his turn he would be too angry to probe beneath the surface and eveal how fragile her defence really was.

They were in London before he said, 'Where do you

want me to drop you—at your father's, or your aunt's?

She said tonelessly, 'Take me to the house, please.' Sh smiled tightly. 'Best to get it over with, as quickly a possible.'

'Oh, yes,' he said very drily. 'Much the best. With an luck you'll soon be able to pretend that none of it eve happened at all.'

He didn't speak again. He even fetched her case fror the boot in silence, and only nodded as she said rathe helplessly, 'Well—goodbye.'

She watched the car go down the street and turn th corner, and felt something die inside her. She still ha her key, so she let herself in. Mrs Lambert was crossin the hall, carrying a tray with a decanter and some glasse and she started so violently on seeing Briony that sh nearly let the whole tray fall to the ground.

'It's all right.' Briony forced a reassuring smile to he lips. 'It—it's not a ghost. It's really me.'

'Miss Briony—but what are you doing here? S Charles said—we thought ...' Mrs Lambert stared ne vously past Briony. 'Are you alone?'

'Yes, quite alone.' Briony closed the door behind he and picked up her case. 'I presume Daddy has been ente taining.'

'Some Americans,' Mrs Lambert said almost mechani ally. She was frowning in utter bewilderment. 'And you room's not ready. Why didn't you let us know? You se Miss Briony, we thought ...'

'I know what you thought.' Briony moistened her lip 'I don't want to go into details at the moment, but you'r quite right. I was—married yesterday. But my husban isn't here with me, and I'm not expecting him. So m old room will be fine. Perhaps you'd let my father kno I'm here.'

She walked into the spacious drawing room. It was pe

ection as usual, not an ornament out of place, not a
allen flower petal to disturb its pristine surface. Not the
leal environment for the return of a prodigal daughter,
riony decided ironically as she looked round her. It was
lmost as if she had never been away, never cracked
ie smooth tenor of life in this house.

She sat down on the edge of a sofa as if she was a
isitor, and presently Mrs Lambert came in with a tray
f coffee and a plate of smoked salmon sandwiches, and
ie news that she had informed Sir Charles of Briony's
nexpected arrival.

'What did he say?' For obvious reasons they had not
opped to eat on the journey, and Briony suddenly
ealised that she was ravenously hungry as she reached
or a sandwich.

'Oh, Miss Briony!' There might almost have been tears
Mrs Lambert's eyes. 'He looked overwhelmed, really
e did—delighted. He's been so unhappy, it's been dread-
ul to see him.'

If Briony had harboured any doubts about her recep-
on, they were dispelled as soon as Sir Charles came into
ie room.

'My darling girl, you're home!' His arms closed round
er fiercely. 'No, don't talk, don't say anything just yet.
here'll be plenty of time for explanations later. Tomor-
ow—when you're rested. You look exhausted.' His tone
ardened. 'That degenerate swine! I'll ...'

'No, Daddy.' Gently, Briony released herself. 'There's
o need for you to do anything. I've left Logan, it's true,
nd later on I'll be applying for an annulment.'

'An annulment?' Sir Charles stared at her as if he did
ot believe his ears. 'Oh, my darling child, thank heavens
ou've been spared that at least!'

Briony smiled. 'I've been spared nothing,' she said,
most conversationally. 'But you're quite right, I am

very tired. If my room's ready, I would like to lie down.'

'Of course, of course.' He was soothing, expansive. His delight in her return was almost tangible, as was his ill-concealed air of triumph. But he refrained from the actual words 'I told you so.'

Briony slept badly that night, and awoke dreading the *tête-à-tête* that she feared her father would force on her, but when she went downstairs she learned he had been called away early to U.P.G. where there was a threatened dispute with the print unions over manning levels, so she was spared.

She spent a desultory day around the house, reading magazines supplied by Mrs Lambert, and watching television, something she normally never did in the daytime. It was from the television news in the early evening that she learned that the dispute at U.P.G. had developed into an all-out strike, and that both sides were taking stances behind rather inflammatory statements.

She despised herself for the thought, but she could not help a slight feeling of relief. With a full-blooded strike on his hands, Sir Charles would have enough problems on his mind for the next few days, and his erring daughter's matrimonial tangle would have to be relegated to the bottom of his list of priorities.

Perhaps by the time the strike was over, some miracle would have happened and she would have grown some kind of extra skin to help her bear her father's inevitable gloating at least with equanimity. For everyone's sake, it was best to make him think that Logan and she had realised at once they were not compatible, and had parted on good terms.

But even with her father's long absences, the days which followed were far from easy. Briony found herself wandering from room to room, unable to settle or to take any real interest in anything. Mrs Lambert, meaning to

›e kind, insisted on treating her as if she was some kind ›f invalid, and, worst of all, there was a visit from Aunt ·Ies to face.

'Child, are you out of your mind?' was her aunt's ·orthright greeting, as she came into the drawing room.

Briony flushed, evading her gaze. 'I don't think so.)idn't you once tell me when I was quite small that the ›ravest thing to do when you made a serious mistake was ıcknowledge the fact and try to put it right?'

'I gave altogether too much advice,' Aunt Hes said rimly. 'And probably I never expected any of it to be aken. Isn't that the main purpose of advice—to be gnored?' She sat down and gave Briony a long look. You're miserable,' she said, half to herself. 'The light hat was on inside you has gone out.'

'I don't know what you mean.'

'I think you do. You were living in my flat before you narried him, my dear. I saw how it was with you. You vanted him—you couldn't hide it. Are you trying to tell ne it was all self-deception, because I warn you, I don't ›elieve it.'

'Perhaps I did. Perhaps I do.' Briony got up feverishly nd walked over to the window. 'I—I can't talk about it ıow.'

Aunt Hes sighed softly. 'So Charles Trevor wins as ısual.'

'Daddy had nothing to do with it,' said Briony, and hen paused, remembering Logan's jeering words. 'At east ...'

'At the very least,' her aunt agreed. 'He likes to remain n full control, does Charles. That's why he's up to his ars in strikes and disputes at this moment, and we both now it. He creates discord at all levels so that he can ·merge victorious. But I thought you knew that. I hought you understood, and that's why you left home and sought a measure of independence for yourself. That's why when I met the man you'd chosen, I was pleased, because I knew that he'd stand up to Charles. She shook her head. 'I assumed, of course, that you'd be fighting for him, not against him.'

'That's not fair,' Briony protested. She could feel tears pricking in her eyes, and was glad her back was turned. 'You—you don't know what happened.'

'I could make an educated guess,' Aunt Hes retorted. 'Come and see me, child, when you're calmer and can think more rationally. You don't have to tell me anything. We won't even mention it again, if that's what you want. And forgive me if I've been interfering. You're my sister's girl, and I'm fond of you—call that my excuse.' She went to the door. 'I was beginning to be fond of your Logan too,' she said, almost musingly, and went out.

Another week limped by, and the strike was clearly no closer to being settled. In early news interviews, Sir Charles had spoken scathingly of the unions and prophesied an unconditional surrender, but now he was beginning to look almost harassed, his immaculate, invincible façade showing distinct signs of wear and tear. He came home to snatch fragments of sleep and the odd meal, and Briony and Mrs Lambert found themselves conferring worriedly over the lines of strain now prominent on his face.

'Worry accumulates,' Mrs Lambert said gloomily one day as she and Briony sat planning a dinner that Sir Charles would probably not be there to eat. 'And poor Sir Charles has had a lot to contend with recently.' She flushed hastily as she caught Briony's eye. 'Oh, I beg your pardon, Miss Briony. I didn't mean—it wasn't that so much as—well, I suppose I shouldn't be discussing this with you.' She sat in silence for a moment looking embarrassed and uncomfortable while Briony waited in some surprise. Mrs Lambert had been a part of the household for as long as she could remember, always self-effacing and discreet, and never one for confidences either about herself or anyone else that Briony could think of.

'Please go on,' she said at last. 'If there's something else bothering my father apart from this wretched strike, it might be best if I knew about it.'

'Oh, I think it's all over with,' Mrs Lambert said quickly. 'Although it can't have been pleasant for him.' She sat for a minute, twisting her fingers together. 'It was one of his lady-friends,' she said awkwardly at last.

'I see.' Briony's amazement increased. This was indiscretion with a vengeance! 'You mean—Fiona de Bruce?'

'Oh, no, Miss Briony. Mrs de Bruce is a very pleasant ady—and the last one to make any kind of—of fuss. This particular person—she wasn't here many times at ll. I never even knew her name. When she came to the ouse, she came with Sir Charles. And they dined out, not ere. Then they would come back to the house and Sir Charles would ask me to take coffee and liqueurs to his tudy.' Mrs Lambert looked distressed. 'That's when I ealised what had been going on. I had the tray awkvardly one night—the last time she came here—and I ouldn't help hearing what they were saying as I put it lown so that I could knock.' She paused.

'Go on,' Briony said, frowning.

'She was laughing, Miss Briony, but not a nice sort of augh at all, and she said, "It'll cost you." Just like that. nd I listened, I'm afraid, because I had this awful feelng that she might be a blackmailer and Sir Charles might eed a witness against her.'

'It's all right,' Briony said gently. 'Please go on.'

'And Sir Charles said "I don't care how much it costs.

Will this be enough to satisfy you?" Then she laughed again and she said, "My God, when you want to be rid of someone, you don't mess about do you?" And he said, "Just as long as I am rid, that's all." And I felt dreadful then, because I realised that she must have become a nuisance, and he was having to buy her off.' Mrs Lambert's face was crimson. 'Such an awful thing to happen and she wasn't at all Sir Charles' type. I knew that as soon as I saw her.'

'What was she like?' Briony's curiosity had been aroused by the unpleasant little story. She thought back over her father's numerous conquests in some perplexity. She had never wondered how his little affairs began or ended, but she would never have imagined he would have to use a cheque book in order to get out of an unwanted liaison.

'Thin,' Mrs Lambert said. 'And neurotic, I thought. Smart, I suppose, in a way, but not a lady.' She hesitated. 'I knocked and took the tray in and put it on the desk in between them. The cheque was still lying there. She hadn't bothered to pick it up, and I couldn't help seeing how much it was for.'

'How much?' Briony queried automatically. What was the selling price for a discarded mistress, who didn't want to go, in Sir Charles' sophisticated little world? she wondered rather bitterly.

Mrs Lambert told her.

'*What?*' Briony heard her voice rise to a squeak. 'You must have made a mistake!'

'No, Miss Briony.' Mrs Lambert sounded positive. 'I could hardly believe it myself, so I had another look, and then Madam saw me and picked up the cheque and stuffed it into her handbag, and Sir Charles said that was all, and they didn't want to be disturbed again, so I came out.' She sighed. 'But your father hasn't been himself since. It's as if he's had something on his mind all the time—apart from missing you, of course,' she added conscientiously.

'Of course,' Briony echoed drily. 'Thank you, Mrs Lambert. You were quite right to tell me.'

But for the rest of the day she found herself wondering just what she had been told. None of it seemed to make any sense. And Mrs Lambert had been quite correct when she had said that this strange woman had not been Sir Charles' usual type. He liked the Fiona de Bruces of this world, either divorced or widowed, with money of their own and figures as opulent as their backgrounds. Someone thin and neurotic would not appeal to his taste at all—unless she had some hold over him.

Now stop it, Briony chided herself. These were realms of fantasy, and she knew it. It was Logan and his tales of bribery and corruption who had started her thinking along these lines. And the maddening thing was she could never ask her father about the woman, without betraying Mrs Lambert.

On an impulse she went along to her father's study and looked in. It seemed the same as it always had, a rather severe and workmanlike room, not at all a background for the ending of a love affair, no matter how acrimonious it might have become. And Daddy must have been desperate to pay out the sort of money Mrs Lambert had mentioned.

She walked over to the desk and stood there for a moment, an inward struggle going on over what she should do next. One inner voice told her not to meddle, that it was none of her affair, and she had troubles of her own. But another, more insistent voice said that this was a mystery that needed solving.

Despising herself, she began to try the drawers of the desk, one by one. Her father's cheque book was normally kept in the top right-hand drawer, and after a brief search she found it. All the stubs were neatly filled in, except one which had been left blank—by accident or design? she wondered. None of the filled-in stubs were made out to a woman or for the amount Mrs Lambert had mentioned. She replaced the cheque book, and began looking in the other drawers—for what, she wasn't sure. But when she saw the manilla folder, half hidden under some papers in the bottom drawer, then she was sure. It was a curious sensation—like the pricking of thumbs, she supposed. And the rest of the quotation jumped into her brain as she laid the folder on the desk. 'Something wicked this way comes.'

And when the press cuttings on the Harry Chapman suicide spilled out of the folder, it was as if she had always known they would be there.

Briony began to tremble. She sank down into the chair behind the desk and looked at the cuttings. Many of them were the same that Marina Chapman had brought to the cottage. Were these the duplicates she had spoken of? Or—more likely from the appearance of the file—were these the U.P.G. collection of cuttings on the case from the office library where she herself had worked?

A thin, neurotic woman, smart but not a lady. Mrs Lambert's description ran through her head with a terrible emphasis. *'My God, when you want to be rid of someone, you don't mess about, do you?' 'Just as long as I am rid, that's all.'*

Not a payment to rid him of a woman who had become an embarrassment, but a bribe—to someone who would readily understand such things. Someone who knew about corruption. The widow of a corrupt man now living comfortably in tax exile on the proceeds of that corruption.

Logan had wondered what could have brought her

rom Jersey all the way to Yorkshire. Well, now she :new. It was money. Sir Charles had been fully aware of vhere they were intending to spend their honeymoon. 'hat was how Marina Chapman had known how to find hem so easily—something she had never really ques-ioned before, although she had not really been in any fit tate to question very much at all. Which her father, of ourse, would have relied on.

But to pay out all that money, she thought, appalled, vith no guarantee that the plan would work. I might ave just shown her the door. He must have been very ure what I would do.

And something flat and cold inside her replied, 'He vas.'

She was still sitting there when he came home several ours later. She heard his arrival, the impatience of his oice as he called for her. There was a note of triumph here too, and she guessed that the strike had been ettled, and on favourable terms to the U.P.G. board. She :new that suppressed jubilance.

At last he tracked her down. 'Are you there, Briony?' Ie peered across the room. 'What the devil are you sit-ing in here in the dark for?'

'Licking my wounds,' she said calmly. 'Have you won gain?'

'Just about.' He was making little effort to conceal his lation. Charles Trevor—Fleet Street's union basher in nother victory performance. 'Get dressed up, my dar-ing, and we'll go and celebrate.' His hand reached for he light switch and clicked it on. Briony saw him look t her, register her white, frozen face, then look down at he desk, as if he too knew what he would see. She saw he guilt, followed closely by the annoyance at his own lumsiness in not returning the file to the library. If e'd done so, she realised, she would never have known.

She put out a hand and touched the file. 'When were you planning to celebrate this victory?' she asked. 'When I received my annulment decree?'

'I know how it must seem,' he began quickly.

'There is no "seem".' She shook her head. 'I know how it is. I know you paid that woman to come to Yorkshire and ruin my honeymoon. She did a fantastic job, didn't she? Even you couldn't have hoped that I would actually leave Logan.' She laughed. 'Lucky Daddy!'

'I did it for your sake,' he said, and quite suddenly he didn't look like the successful chairman of a giant publishing conglomerate. He looked tired and elderly. 'You couldn't be happy with that man. He wasn't fit to marry you. Everyone knows my opinion of journalists. Can you imagine what I went through? The things in other newspapers? The jokes and snide remarks in my own offices that I wasn't supposed to hear. Everyone was laughing at me.'

'And that was what mattered most,' she said.

'No!' He was vehement. 'All I ever wanted was for you to be happy, my darling. And you couldn't be happy with him. Why, he was having an affair with that Wellesley woman when you first met. I know her type. She wouldn't have allowed a little thing like his marriage to you to get in her way. You'd have sat alone night after night, wondering where he was, who he was with. You'd have been a novelty at first—someone innocent to make love to—and *my* daughter, which would have added an extra spice for him.'

'Perhaps you're right,' she sighed. 'Perhaps everything you say is true. But I would still have had the chance of some happiness first. Your way—I've had nothing but misery.'

She stood up.

'Where are you going?' he said sharply.

'To Logan.' She did not look at him. She put the cuttings back in the file and replaced them exactly as she had found them. 'To tell him what you did, and ask him to forgive me, if he can.'

'Of course he'll forgive you,' Sir Charles said roughly. 'He'd be a fool not to. He'll stay married to you for as long as it suits him—while he collects the dossier of information which will take him the next step up the ladder. That's why Mackenzie hired him, you know—because of his investigation into the Chapman business. You were still at school when it all happened. You're only a child now. You don't know men like Logan Adair. You don't know anything about the kind of world they inhabit. I wanted to protect you from that.'

'You talk of protection,' she said slowly. 'You also mentioned a dossier of information. Just whom are you afraid Logan might conduct his next investigative campaign against, Daddy? You?'

She only put the barest necessities into her overnight bag. She could collect the rest of her things tomorrow, she thought. All that mattered now was seeing Logan and trying to put things right between them.

She felt sick and nervous as she stood outside the door to the flat. It had been planned that Logan and she should live there after the honeymoon, and Tony had moved elsewhere. She hoped that Logan had not asked him to move back again. The last thing she wanted at a moment like this was any kind of audience.

Once before she had stood here with shaking hands and rung this bell, she thought. And the wait for a response had seemed endless then too.

The door opened at last, and Briony's little speech so agonisingly rehearsed over and over again in the taxi which had brought her here died on her lips as she saw who was standing in the doorway.

'Good God!' Karen Wellesley said at last. 'The blushing bride herself!' Her eyes fell on Briony's overnight case, and her catlike smile widened. 'If you've decided this is reconciliation time, ducky, then you've picked a bad moment.'

Briony looked at her. Karen's hair was tousled, and even the most casual observer would have known that she wore nothing at all under her loosely fastened bathrobe.

Briony moistened her lips. 'Nevertheless, I'd like to speak to Logan, please,' she said, trying to sound cool, as if she was quite used to trying to reach him past the hostile figures of semi-naked women.

'Impossible, I'm afraid.' Karen's eyes never left her face. 'He's asleep, and he wouldn't take very kindly to being woken up, I can promise you.' She smiled with provocative reminiscence. 'He's had a very exhausting time just lately, poor sweet. I'm sure you understand me. Why don't I just tell him you called, and let him get in touch with you later—if he wants to.' She emphasised the 'if' very slightly, and smiled again.

'On second thoughts,' Briony said very calmly, 'let's just forget the whole thing, shall we? And thank you for making the situation so clear. I was in grave danger of making an utter fool of myself.'

'Oh, it was hardly that bad.' Karen's voice was like syrup. 'You're just a little out of your depth, that's all. You were from the start. Goodnight, Miss Trevor.'

But Briony had already turned away. She did not want the additional humiliation of having Karen Wellesley shut Logan's door in her face.

She never expected to see him again. Her father made no comment about her unexpected return home, and she offered no explanation. Logan and her marriage became taboo subjects by tacit understanding.

Nothing very much seemed to matter any more, so she decided she might as well conform to the pattern that her father had laid down. She enrolled for a Cordon Bleu cookery course. She arranged flowers, and she became a demure and charming hostess. When he introduced young men to her, most of them rising executives from the ranks of U.P.G. itself, she accepted their inevitable invitations politely. Sometimes she felt she had become a marionette ready to dance to whatever string anyone chose to pull.

But she made no move towards obtaining her annulment, for reasons she wasn't even prepared to discuss with herself. There had been a small flurry of interest in the Press about the failure of her marriage, and even some cynical hints that the whole unlikely match had been a publicity stunt arranged by Sir Charles Trevor for some devious reason of his own. She didn't want to arouse that interest again by applying for an annulment, when she could divorce Logan after two years' separation without attracting very much attention at all.

She couldn't avoid all mention of him, of course. He still wrote for the *Courier*, and she had the pain of seeing his byline when she unfolded the paper. But each time, she told herself, the pain grew less. It was as if she was learning slowly how to distance herself from everything that had happened.

She had reverted to the use of her maiden name, but had not removed her wedding ring, an anomaly which she guessed Sir Charles found it difficult to understand. But it was never mentioned. Relegated to the cupboard along with the rest of the skeletons, she thought cynically.

She was gaining a reputation for extreme coolness, she

knew. Very few of her dates, having undergone an evening of her quiet politeness, ever asked her again, and she was content for this to be so. She wanted no lovemaking, no attempt at any kind of physical relationship. She was afraid of it, because she could remember only too clearly the wild response which Logan had ignited, and which must never be allowed to happen again because it made her too vulnerable.

It was at a dinner party at the London house that she first heard the impending trouble in Azabia being discussed. She knew very little about the place, except that it produced oil and was ruled by a despotic sheik who was amicably disposed towards the West. But all that, she heard, was due to change at any moment, as it had in other oil-producing countries, and no one knew exactly what the new régime would be or what its policies would be aimed against. It was then that someone inadvertently mentioned Logan. There was an immediate embarrassed silence and an instant change of subject.

Later Briony tackled her father. 'Is there going to be some kind of uprising in Azabia? A war?'

He shrugged evasively. 'It's a little premature to state definitely that anything's going to happen there, but there are—indications.'

Indications. Briony lay awake that night and considered. It had seemed from the discussion over dinner that a revolution was a certainty and in the not too distant future. And it was obvious that Logan was being sent by the *Courier* to report on the troubles from Azabia almost from their inception, all of which spelled danger.

She thought, 'Why should I care? I don't even want to care. Let Karen Wellesley worry about what happens to him. They're probably together at this moment, bidding each other a fond farewell. I'm mad even to give him a second thought.'

But the events of the following evening forced her to do more than just think.

She had been to a rather dull party and had left early and alone. She was standing on the step, trying to fit her latchkey into the door, when a hand reached over her shoulder and took it from her. At the same time an arm like an iron clamp fastened round her waist propelling her forwards through the opening door. She was too breathless, too surprised to scream, even when she turned to see who her assailant was.

'Your key, darling,' Logan said pleasantly, and tossed it to her.

'Get out of here!' she whispered.

'Presently.' He nodded towards the drawing room. 'We'll talk in there.'

'We have nothing to say to each other.'

'Not even goodbye?' he asked sardonically, and smiled as he saw her flush. 'I guessed the word of my impending departure would have got around by now. I see I was right. Aren't you going to wish me luck in Azabia? I've the strangest feeling I'm going to need it.'

'You can manage without my good wishes, Logan,' she said coldly. 'You can make your own luck.'

'Then I can only hope the recent happenings in my life aren't a sample of it,' he said drily.

'I wouldn't have said you had a great deal to complain about.' Her heartbeat was fluttering like a panic-stricken bird, but she managed to face him inimically.

'And what's that supposed to mean?' He raised his eyebrows.

'Make of it what you will. Now will you please go?'

'Not without what I came for,' he answered calmly.

'Which is?'

'Among other things, this.' One unhurried stride brought him to her, and it was too late to cry out, or run away or do any of the things she should have done at the very beginning of this preposterous confrontation, because his mouth was on hers, hard and warm and searching, and her body was locked against his as if she had been magnetised. When he eventually released her, her mouth felt bruised and she was on the point of collapse. He put her at arm's length and studied her as if she was some kind of curious scientific specimen.

'Interesting,' he said at last. 'And could become more so, I suspect. What a pity I have a plane to catch.'

'You lay another finger on me,' she raged, aware of her flushed face and hectically flurried breathing, 'and I'll ...'

'You'll what? Scream for Daddy to rescue you, I suppose. Except that I happen to know that Daddy is otherwise engaged this evening. A Mrs de Bruce, I understand. And it's the housekeeper's evening off, too, so I might just go ahead and let you scream.'

'Don't you dare to touch me!'

'Why not?' he asked derisively. 'I'm not one of Daddy's tame boardroom trainees. I'm your husband, remember? Or do you need a more permanent reminder?'

'No!' she panted, and wrenched herself free, wiping her hand savagely across her swollen mouth as if such a gesture could erase the marks of his passion.

'You're a little hypocrite, Briony, but unfortunately I haven't time to teach you the depths of your own hypocrisy. I have to get to the airport.'

'Then go!' She was shaking, partly in anger and partly through some other emotion which she could neither understand nor explain.

'When I get what I came for,' he said. 'I want to hear you say that you love me.'

'You must be mad,' she said, after an astonished pause.

'I think I was,' he said. 'To let you get away from me so

easily. But I don't intend to let you go again. Now tell me that you love me and that you'll be waiting for me when I get back from Azabia.'

'Go to hell,' she said very slowly and distinctly.

'I'll come back from there too, if I have to,' he said. 'Now say the words to me, Briony. It doesn't even matter if you don't mean them at the moment. I'll attend to that when I come back.'

'You mean if you come back, don't you?' she said with all the cruelty she could muster. 'Please don't bother on my account, Logan. You're not the only one who's found consolation. Now, will you get out?'

He was staring at her as if he had never seen her before, the aquamarine eyes narrowed and incredulous. Then he gave a swift, shaken laugh. 'Yes, I'll go,' he said. 'And gladly, you little bitch.'

The front door slammed behind him. Briony made her way slowly over to the foot of the stairs and sank down on to the bottom step, clinging on to the elegant curve of the newel post as a drowning man might cling to a piece of wreckage. After a long time she heard herself cry out—a sound that might have been his name.

CHAPTER SIX

A STRANGE grey light was filtering into the room when Briony awoke. For a moment she could not work out where she was—then everything came rushing back to her. She had disarranged the curtains slightly in her wanderings the night before and she could see that although no snow was actually falling at the moment, the clouds were full of it.

She shivered, huddling further under the covers for a warmth she did not find. Presently she would have to get up and dress and go downstairs, and it was not a prospect she relished. Or, she supposed, she could stay there in bed and not go down at all, except that hunger would drive her down eventually, even if Logan didn't.

His arrival the previous night still seemed like a figment of a nightmare, but she was awake now, and the bad dream like the snow was still there and threatening her.

She sighed. It was a horrible coincidence that they should both have chosen the same bolt-hole, but it was no more than that, and as it was certain that neither of them could get away immediately, then the only thing was to bear the situation as gracefully as possible.

Two civilised people, she began—and then stopped. There had been very little that was civilised about her relationship with Logan since their ill-fated wedding. She couldn't rely on civilisation to get her out of this mess. For the first time, she regretted that the cottage wasn't on the telephone, always supposing the lines were still working. She would have been tempted to phone London and persuade Christopher to come in a helicopter and rescue her.

Christopher. She winced slightly. There was another problem. She knew now that she had allowed herself to think back over the past year that her feelings for him were lukewarm at best. And yet he was confidently expecting her to divorce Logan and marry him as soon as possible. It was to escape his none-too-subtle promptings as well as her father's that she had fled.

And why had she run away? To think, that was why. To clear her mind and decide what she had to do. What it was best for her to do. And all she had succeeded in doing was recalling a lot of memories which would have best been left buried in her subconscious, and muddling herself completely. She hardly knew who she was any more, let alone what she wanted.

She glanced at her watch and grimaced. It was already past nine o'clock, and time she presented herself downstairs. The last thing she wanted was Logan coming in search of her. She got out of bed and put on her housecoat and slippers, then went along to the bathroom. In spite of its size it was more like a refrigerator than anything else, but the water in the taps was warm and Briony reminded herself that she should be thankful for small mercies.

Back in her room, she hesitated for a moment over her choice of clothes, before deciding to wear the jeans and sweater she had arrived in. She had more feminine clothes with her, but her femininity was something she wanted to understate in the present situation.

As she went downstairs she could hear the sound of Logan's typewriter tapping away furiously behind the closed door of the parlour. It seemed he really had come there to write.

The living room fire was burning steadily, well banked up with logs and small coal, and when Briony had made herself some coffee, she carried it to the chair by the fire. It was going, she thought grimly, to be a long day.

It began snowing again about an hour later, and she watched the feathery flakes whirling down with renewed dismay. She'd never been to the cottage so late in the year before, so she had no real idea how bad things could get, but it seemed as if they might be snowed up here for days, if not weeks. She stifled a groan at the thought, then tensed because she had heard the parlour door open. She snatched a book from the shelf beside the fireplace and was sitting, apparently absorbed in reading, when the living room door opened and Logan came in.

'Good morning.' His tone was as casual as if they had been strangers staying in the same hotel, she thought furiously. 'I'm going to make some coffee. Do you want some?'

'I've just had a cup, thanks.' She was aware how stilted her voice sounded.

'As you wish.' He went through into the kitchen whistling softly through his teeth and she heard him filling the kettle and switching it on. She'd imagined he would remain out there while he waited for it to boil, so his voice just behind her came as a shock, and she jumped.

'Good book?' he inquired conversationally.

'Excellent.'

'An old favourite of yours? One that you know well?'

'Not particularly. Why?' She didn't even know what it was. She had just grabbed the nearest and opened it without looking.

'Because you have it upside down,' he said smoothly. He reached over her shoulder, took the book from her nerveless hand and gave it back to her the right way up.

'Thank you,' she said, quivering with temper.

'Not at all.' He whistled appreciatively. '*My Spiritual Mission among the Indians of the Amazon Basin* by the Reverend Bertram Gleason,' he read aloud. 'Perhaps you'd prefer it the way it was.'

She smiled pallidly, mentally consigning both him and the unknown missionary to a hotter place than the Amazon basin. For a few moments she was desperately aware of him still standing behind her chair, then at last he moved away back into the kitchen and she relaxed visibly.

When Logan came back with his coffee, she was standing by the window.

'I think it's getting worse,' she said bleakly.

'I'm sure it is.' He gulped down some of the hot coffee, wincing slightly. 'The forecast is bad too.'

'You've heard it?'

'I brought a radio with me.' He crushed the dawning hope in her face. 'But no spare batteries, so I'm afraid I can't offer to lend it to you for your entertainment. There might come a time when we need to hear the forecast or the news.'

'Yes, of course,' she said stiffly. She couldn't tell him that she was almost desperate for some kind of cheerful noise to come between herself and her thoughts. It was so hushed in the cottage, its isolation emphasised by the muffling blanket all around them, that she was conscious of the slightest sound—the dislodgement of a piece of coal in the grate, the tick of the clock, the distant tap of the typewriter. All of them seemed to underline how alone she was, and how unprotected. Which was not a train of thought she had any desire to pursue.

Logan said abruptly, 'What time are we eating?'

'I beg your pardon?'

He sighed impatiently. 'What—time—is—lunch?' he spelled out with unnecessary elaboration.

'Are you expecting me to cook for you?' she demanded indignantly.

He shrugged. 'It seems the most obvious course, unless you're fasting. Look on it as a wifely duty—one of the many you've neglected since our marriage.' He raised an eyebrow. 'Satisfy that one, and I might forgo the others.'

'Please don't make jokes,' she said between her teeth.

'Who said I was joking?' he said pleasantly, and went back to the parlour. She waited for the sound of the typewriter, then she went out of the living room and upstairs to the guest room. The mattress felt cold to the touch, but not damp, and she fetched sheets and blankets and made up a bed. She supposed that by rights she should offer Logan the main bedroom as he was renting the place from her aunt, but judging by the mood he was in this morning that didn't seem a very good idea.

She went down to the kitchen and surveyed the store cupboards. On the face of it, they had plenty of supplies, and when the bread ran out she could always supplement their diet by baking scones and soda bread. It seemed that the down-to-earth cookery lessons she'd been given at school were likely to stand her in better stead here than the course she had undertaken in London.

After some thought, she peeled and boiled some potatoes, then made some pastry, combining the cooked potato and a tin of stewed steak under the pastry crust. Tinned peas would have to do, she decided, dismissing nostalgic thoughts of baby carrots and broccoli spears, and they would have fresh fruit for dessert. There had been some apples and oranges among the provisions delivered by Mrs Barnes the previous night.

When the pie was almost ready she laid a tray with a knife and fork, and added a glass of water, then carried it through to the parlour. For no particular reason that she could define, she knocked before entering, and heard Logan say 'Come in' above the incessant noise of the typewriter.

He glanced at the tray. 'Aren't you eating?'

'Yes. I thought you'd prefer to have yours in here.'

'Then you thought wrong,' he said. He got up from the table and stretched. 'I need a break, anyway.'

She had no choice but to turn and retreat back to the living room, where she had laid a place for herself on the table by the window. Reluctantly, she set Logan's knife and fork in the opposite place, then went to fetch the pie and the vegetables.

She had been hungry, but having to sit at the same table with him destroyed her appetite. She merely picked at her small portion of pie, and hoped he would not notice. He himself ate heartily, she noticed rather crossly.

As he took a second helping he said rather drily, 'I'm sorry if my greed shocks you, Briony, but when I was on the run in Azabia I never knew where my next meal was coming from—or if there was even going to be a next meal.'

She asked, 'Exactly how did you get away, Logan?'

He smiled at her. 'I'll give you a signed copy of the book when it comes out. You can read all about it.'

'You're writing about it, but you don't want to discuss it?' she asked wonderingly.

'That's right.' He took an apple and cut it into quarters. 'You can call the book an exorcism if you like. I hope it will drive my demons away, but I can't be sure.'

She stared at him, taking her first good long look. Really seeing him for the first time since his return. He was thinner, but she'd noticed that before, and all his features seemed more sharply defined in some odd way, their lines harsher and more prominent, as if they had been recast in some deeper and more bitter mould. He looks older, she thought, and bleaker, and yet I surely couldn't have expected him to go through an experience like being on the run with a price on his head and emerge unscathed.

'What are you doing? Seeing if the scars show?' he asked, and she flushed.

'I suppose so. You've—changed.'

'No doubt you feel there was plenty of room for improvement,' he murmured mockingly. 'Do you want me to tell you that you've changed too?'

She shrugged silently. She wasn't sure she wanted him to tell her anything at all about herself. Personal subjects were best avoided in the circumstances, she thought.

'You're more beautiful, of course,' he said. 'But that was to be expected. You'd be lovelier still if you relaxed more. You have a wary, slightly hunted look about you.'

'How strange,' she said coolly. 'I was thinking exactly the same about you.'

'But I have every reason to look like that.' He finished the last of his apple. 'What's your excuse?'

She collected the dirty plates and took them into the kitchen. Logan followed, lounging in the doorway while she ran water into the sink and added washing up liquid. The water was hotter than she'd intended, and she winced slightly as she snatched at the steaming plates and put them in the drying rack.

'You should wear gloves,' Logan said abruptly. He came across to her side. 'You'll spoil your hands ...' His voice broke off and she saw that he was looking at the bareness of her left hand. Briony heard herself swallow. In the silence of the kitchen, it seemed a deafening sound.

He took her hand and studied it. 'You were wearing it,' he said half to himself. 'It was one of the first things I noticed as you came down the stairs that first night in London. And now you're not. Why?'

'Does it matter?' She twisted out of his grasp, reaching for a towel to dry her hands, making sure there was several feet of space between them.

'Of course it bloody matters! While you thought you were a widow you wore your ring. Now you know that you're still a wife, you've taken it off. It makes no sense.'

She shrugged again. 'Perhaps I wore it out of respect —or habit. I really can't remember.' But she'd been aware of it all the time, she thought, and more than aware of how much Christopher and her father hated seeing it on her hand. She had supposed that if she accepted Christopher's proposal and his ring, then she would transfer Logan's wedding ring to her other hand. 'But wearing it now would be sheer hypocrisy,' she went on, lifting her chin as she met his narrowed gaze. 'I'm not your wife, Logan, and I never have been. We went through a ceremony together, that was all.'

'Don't you dare say that was all!' The aquamarine eyes were blazing now. 'I remember, even if you don't, how it was with us as we drove here that day. God in heaven, Briony, you melted into my arms, and your mouth tasted like all the roses that have ever been since the beginning of time.'

'Please stop it,' she said sharply. 'There's no point in talking like that. We were different people then.'

He said quietly, 'I don't think the changes have been all that fundamental.'

She read his intention in his face and tried to duck past him, out of the kitchen. She had some vague notion of locking herself into her room, but it was too late. Logan had been strong before, but now his muscles felt like whipcord as he dragged her into his arms.

She gasped chokingly, imploringly, 'No—you mustn't!' Then all further protests were wiped away as his mouth took hers. Bracing her hands against his chest, she tried with all her might to push him away, but it was useless, and all she achieved was a disturbing awareness of the warmth of his body through the wool sweater. His mouth teased subtly, sliding along her lips, coaxing them apart, then possessed, exploring the contours of her mouth with deliberate sensuality, drinking her sweetness, draining her until the kitchen seemed to swing in a dizzying arc, and she closed her eyes, lost to everything but Logan, the scent and the feel of him.

He had been holding her half-pinioned in his arms so

that she could not struggle or take flight. But now his hands moved, sliding down over the smooth rounded line of her hips, urging her body forward until it ground against his in yet another form of kiss.

He said hoarsely against her mouth, 'Touch me, Briony. For God's sake, I need to feel your hands on me.'

She slid her hands under his sweater. His body felt hard, the muscles taut across his chest and abdomen, but his skin was like silk and she caressed it with her finger-tips, tracing out a teasing pathway of her own across his ribs, and up to his shoulders, then lightly across his shoulder blades and down the arch of his spinal column.

He groaned softly, pleasurably, and kissed her again, long and lingeringly as if the softness of her lips was some previously unexplored terrain which he proposed to chart in full. His hands pushed the sweater away from the waistband of her jeans, and moved upwards, their sensuous progress impeded only for the second it took him to deal with the clip fastening of her bra. Free of their restraint, her breasts swelled, eager for his hands to cup them, his mouth to take whatever toll of her he wished.

A sudden shudder ran through her as she realised exactly the path she was travelling with him so willingly. She forced her eyes open, as if she was waking from a drugged sleep.

'No,' she managed. She took a step backwards away from him. 'Just stop right there!'

Logan said huskily, 'You don't want to stop, Briony, any more than I do. The difference in us is the same as it's always been. You're female and I'm male.'

She took another step backwards and he watched, his brows drawing together angrily.

He said, 'Briony, you're my wife, and I want you.'

She said, forcing herself to calmness and control, 'Am I supposed to feel flattered?' She shook her head. 'If I was anyone's wife, and we were stuck together in a cottage out in the wilds, you'd want me. I'm not the little innocent I was in such matters, Logan. I don't believe in the one man–one woman bit any more, for which I have you to thank.'

'I suppose you know what you're talking about, because I'm damned if I do!' His voice was harsh. He was fighting for his self-control and against his anger, she guessed.

'It's not important.' She hesitated. 'You wanted to know why I'm not wearing your ring. It's because I've met someone else. I'm engaged to him.'

There was a long silence. It crackled along her nerve endings, and she stared down at the floor, not daring to look up and see what was in his face.

At last he'd said, 'I'd say the engagement was a—little premature. You're supposed to dispose of one husband before moving on to the next.'

'That's understood, of course.' She moved her shoulders nervously. 'I—I wouldn't actually announce anything until the divorce goes through in a year or so.'

'Or more,' he said coolly. 'Depending whether or not I agree to it.'

She did look up then, her eyes indignant. 'What's that supposed to mean?'

'You take a lot for granted, sweet wife,' he said. 'You mention divorce and assume my consent.'

Her heart was thudding slow and heavy against her ribs. She said, 'This is ridiculous! You must want to be free as much as I do.'

'Eventually, maybe.' He smiled, but not a pleasant smile. Her mouth went dry. 'But please don't bandy the word "free" about in my presence. I've learned only recently just how precious a commodity it is, and our views on it might not coincide.'

'I see.' Her growing nervousness made her reckless. 'Well, perhaps I won't bother about a divorce, after all. Perhaps I'll go for an annulment, as I originally intended.'

'On the grounds of non-consummation, I take it.' His smile widened. 'You do take a lot for granted, my sweet. As you reminded me, we're a man and a woman stuck together in a cottage in the wilds, and I've already demonstrated the fact that I want you. So don't rely on my latent chivalry to protect you. I'm guaranteeing nothing.'

Briony drew a long shaking breath. 'Well, at least we know where we stand,' she said, and walked past him out of the kitchen.

All the way across the living room, along the hall and up the stairs, she was listening, her nerves jumping in panic, for the sound of him coming after her, but she was still alone when she reached her room, pushing the door closed behind her, and sagging in relief against its elderly panels, trying to steady her ragged breathing.

Presently she reached down behind her, her fingers searching for the key. It would only provide her with a fragile barricade, but it was better than nothing, and it would give her sadly dented morale a boost. But all she found was an empty lock.

She turned disbelievingly and stared at the door, but only to confirm the bad news her seeking fingers had already conveyed. The key had gone.

But it had been there the night before, she knew it had.

Logan, she thought, and her hand crept up to touch her cheek. He had been up here, probably while she was making that damned pie, and taken the key from the door.

So everything which had happened between them in

he kitchen had been carefully planned, she thought uriously, and the theft of the key was extra insurance ust in case he hadn't been able to instantly seduce his way into her room.

The accusation that she had flung at him that any woman would do under the circumstances had been deiberately aimed to hurt him, but it had rebounded on her. There was no other woman but herself, and he had nade quite sure that he had uninterrupted access to her, and that she knew it.

She went across to the bed and sat down on the edge of it, wrapping her arms defensively across her body.

She had no other defences against him. He had proved hat more than conclusively just now when she had been unable to hide the yearning that his kisses and caresses had woken in her body.

And she knew that if he'd said he loved her, and not nerely that he wanted her, she would have been his for he taking.

t was twilight when she heard his footsteps on the stairs. She tensed involuntarily, hoping that he would walk past on his way to the bathroom, but her door opened, and Logan stood there, a dimly seen figure in the gathering darkness.

He said, 'This room's like the interior of an iceberg. There's a good fire and some supper waiting for you downstairs.' There was a pause, then he said roughly, Are you going to walk, or do I have to carry you?'

Briony stood up, stretching her cramped limbs. 'I can walk, thank you,' she said coolly and distinctly.

'Then do so.' His tone matched hers.

The living room had never appeared so cheerful. The curtains were drawn and the fire was roaring up the chimney. The lamps had been lit, but not the overhead light, which added to the intimacy of the atmosphere.

'Egg and chips,' Logan said briefly, and put them in front of her. 'And you damned well eat them. I saw the way you picked at your lunch, and I've no wish to end up with a sick girl on my hands. I'm here to work, in case you'd forgotten.'

In case *she'd* forgotten! She was stunned by the injustice of the remark, but her reply was hampered by a mouthful of chips. Logan went back to the kitchen and fetched his own plateful. She watched him covertly as she ate. The subdued lighting in the room heightened his already deep tan, making his face look dark and remote. He seemed absorbed in his own thoughts, and she could only hope that she was not the subject of them.

She finished every scrap of the egg and chips, and followed them with two cups of coffee and three chocolate biscuits. Logan lifted a sardonic eyebrow.

'I'm pleased to see that you're not concerned with dieting like most women,' he remarked.

Most women? Did Karen Wellesley have to watch the carbohydrates in order to preserve her elegant figure Briony wondered, and felt her fingers curl into claws at the thought.

She was going to wash the dishes, but Logan waved her away. 'You did the lunch,' he said. 'We'll share the chores and meal-getting. Do you want some more coffee?'

'I don't think so. It might keep me awake,' she said and could have bitten her tongue out. She'd intended to expunge even the remotest reference to bedtime from her conversation. Her face flamed, and Logan gave her a long, dry look before returning to the kitchen.

She was huddled in her chair by the fire, watching the dancing flames rather unhappily when he returned.

'Down to basics,' he said. 'Do you play chess?'

She was startled. 'I know the moves.'

'That's something,' he approved. 'Poker?'

'No—I've never . . .'

'I'll teach you.' He reached into one of the cupboards beside the hearth and brought out a chessboard and a box of pieces. He saw her faintly startled expression and sent her a sardonic smile. 'Innocent diversions, my sweet, to help pass the long winter evenings. Unless you have other plans? No, I thought not.' He handed her the white queen. 'Rather appropriate, don't you think?'

He was a stern teacher, she discovered, with little patience for wandering concentration or ill-thought-out moves. She had played only rarely, largely because her father did not care for chess, but by the end of the evening something of the game's fascination had begun to grip her.

'I enjoyed that,' she confessed as Logan packed the pieces away in the box.

'We aim to please.' He stood up. 'Sure about that coffee?'

'Quite sure.'

He nodded abruptly and went into the kitchen. Presently he returned, carrying a tumbler which he held out to her.

'Warm milk,' he said briefly. 'The perfect soporific, or so I understand—with a dash of whisky to distinguish it from baby food. Make the most of it, because we'll be down to the powdered stuff before too long if this weather holds up.'

'Is it still snowing.' She took the tumbler and sipped appreciatively.

'No, but it's freezing hard.' He took the chair on the opposite side of the hearth, stretching out his long legs to the fire. He looked weary, suddenly, and oddly grim too.

'What are you thinking?' Briony asked.

'About how hot it was in Azabia,' he said. 'I neve
thought I'd see another English winter. Even this blizzar
has seemed like a miracle after that hot, stinking, fly
encrusted hellhole.' He gave a faint laugh. 'Paradoxical
isn't it? It's a confirmation of freedom for me, and a
prison for you. And talking of prisons——' he felt in hi
pocket and produced something which he tossed over t
her. She found herself looking down at the key to he
bedroom. 'This is yours.'

'But I thought——' she began, then stopped.

'You were meant to think,' he said tiredly. 'But what'
the point? You've found another man, and you wer
honest enough to tell me so. If I took you to bed, I'
be cheating him, and while that might give me som
pleasure, I'd also be cheating myself at the same time
Do you understand what I'm trying to say?'

'I think so,' she said. Her mouth was suddenly dry, an
she put the empty tumbler down beside her. She stoo
up, clutching the key. 'Thank—thank you, Logan.'

'I'm sorry you chose this particular place to run to,' h
said. 'You'd have run away again by now, wouldn't you
if it wasn't for the snow.'

'Probably,' she agreed.

'That instinct which led you to run away from me o
our wedding night was probably a right one too.' H
rose to his feet. 'Go to bed, Briony, and if you still sa
your prayers, ask for a quick thaw, preferably beginnin
at midnight.'

She murmured something incoherent and fled.

She lay awake in the darkness for a long time, listen
ing for his step on the stairs, her eyes fixed on the un
locked door. Eventually in the distance she heard th
sound of the typewriter like a chattering tongue, and sh

turned on to her face and lay like a stone with her hands pressed over her ears.

It snowed again in the night, and when she went down-stairs the following morning Logan greeted her with the news that there was no electricity. According to a local radio broadcast, the snow had brought some power lines down, he said, and the supply had been cut off to a number of villages.

'Apparently the drifts are making it difficult for the electricians to get through and repair them,' he added aconically. 'I take it there's some alternative arrangement for cooking?'

'There's a camping stove, yes,' Briony admitted. 'Aunt Hes and I used to use it for picnics. I'm not sure how much bottled gas there'll be, though.'

'Hm.' Logan gave a slight shrug. 'Then we'll have to ation the use of it very strictly. We'd better look out ome candles as well.'

'Then you don't think the power will be on again by onight?'

'I'd say it was doubtful in the extreme. Apparently ven the snow-ploughs are having problems in places.' He gave her a quick glance. 'For God's sake, Briony, don't ook so panic-stricken! We'll survive. I didn't spend a ouple of months of my life dodging Ben Yusef's thugs o come home and freeze to death in an English blizzard.'

'No, of course not,' she said in a stifled voice. She urned away. 'I—I'll go and look for the stove.'

There was a small dry cellar beneath the cottage, ap-proached by a door underneath the stairs. A torch was ept on a ledge just inside the door, and Briony switched this on before making her way down the stone steps. The cellar was as neat as a pin, and it took only a few moments to locate the articles she needed—the stove, an extra cylinder of gas, and a box of candles, but Briony found herself delaying her return to the living room.

There was no way she could admit to Logan that her panic had been caused not by the possible privations they might suffer because of the weather, but through dread of the emotional tension they were living in. It made no sense, she knew that, particularly as Logan had given her his assurance that she had nothing to fear from him.

She didn't doubt him either. But she knew, as he did not, that it was herself she had to fear. That last night in the cold bedroom she had lain awake for hours and ached for him. A small, bitter laugh escaped her lips as she recognised the enormity of the admission.

A slight feeling of compunction invaded her mind at the thought of Christopher whom she had used as a safeguard. She knew now that she would never marry him, no matter what became of her, and that the most she had ever felt for him was affection, and no deeper emotion. She wondered detachedly if it was possible that she might never feel any deeper emotion for any man other than Logan. If this were true, then it was a bleak prospect for the rest of her life.

There would be other Christophers, she supposed vaguely. Suitable young men brought by her father to have dinner at the house, who would ask her to go out with them at his none-too-subtle prompting.

But her father would be disappointed about Christopher. He had been pretty well everything Sir Charles demanded in a son-in-law, she thought—presentable, successful, ambitious for more success, and a fervent admirer of the group Chairman. She had heard her father say on a number of occasions, 'I can always rely on Christopher.'

She had relied on Christopher too. He had been kind and not too demanding in those dark weeks after Logan' death had been reported—a time when Briony had felt she was living two separate lives. On the surface she was calm, dealing coolly with the few embarrassed condolences which had come her way. But underneath, a very different Briony had cried out in anguish for everything she had lost. She would wake in the night, with tears on her face, remembering Logan's last visit to her when he had asked her to tell him that she loved him, and she, encircled by her hurt pride, had sent him away.

Yes, Christopher had been kind, and discreetly attentive, and in a dazed way, behind the cool mask she had presented to the world, she had been grateful to him. And her gratitude might in time have pushed her almost inadvertently into marriage. Numbed and empty as she had felt, with gentle pressure from both Christopher and her father to contend with, how could she have resisted? And then Logan had returned, and the whole world had turned upside down.

'Briony!' His voice from the top of the cellar steps brought her tinglingly back to reality. 'Are you all right? What are you doing?'

'I—I had to search for the stove,' she lied, and began to clamber back up the steps.

'Give those things to me,' he said impatiently. 'Why didn't you call me—tell me what you were up to?' His hand reached out and brushed her hair in a long, lingering movement. She felt herself flinching away involuntarily, and he stiffened.

'You have a cobweb in your hair,' he said coldly. 'Go and look in the mirror if you don't believe me.'

She wanted to cry out that it wasn't a case of not believing. That it was just that his slightest touch had the power to set her physically alight, and she could not allow that to happen again, because if it did she would be completely lost.

Besides, she told herself as she walked back into the living room, it wasn't really what Logan wanted either. His desire for her might have been reawakened because of the circumstances in which they found themselves, but he had other commitments as she knew to her bitter cost.

It was a difficult day, and a long one. Logan checked the stores meticulously, and said there was enough food to keep them going for at least another two weeks, if they were careful. His lips twisted slightly at the sight of the solitary spare gas cylinder, but he merely said it would do until the power lines were repaired again.

But if they're having problems as it is, Briony found herself thinking. And if it goes on snowing . . .

Later Logan went out and dug out a path to the front gate, and just beyond. Briony had offered to help, but he had refused her assistance so curtly that she had not cared to press the matter.

They ate their supper by firelight in order to economise on candles. Briony wondered whether she should suggest another game of chess, but in the shadows cast by the flickering flames Logan's face looked so bitter and remote that she did not dare mention it. After sitting in uncomfortable silence for a while, she said mendaciously that she was tired and intended to have an early night.

The air in the bedroom felt icy and even the hot water bottle she had filled for herself did little to dispel the chill of the sheets. She wondered if Logan intended to spend half the night typing again, but she could hear no sound at all from the ground floor, and presently, to her own surprise, she drifted into sleep.

She awoke with a start and sat up, wondering what had disturbed her. A sound? She strained her ears and heard it again—a moaning sound, rising to a choking cry. Her first thought was that Logan was ill. She was out of bed in a flash, huddling into her housecoat and trying with shaking hands to relight the candle on her bedside table. Then she went across the landing and into his room.

As she went in, he turned on to his back, muttering something, but Briony saw that his eyes were closed. The sheets and blankets on his bed were tumbled and pushed to one side as if he had been tossing and turning for most of the night.

Then she heard him moan again, and the sound sent a shiver cringing down the length of her spine. She put the candle down and bent over him, shaking his bare shoulder insistently.

'Logan, wake up! You're having a bad dream.'

It seemed an age before he opened his eyes, and when he did, he stared at her for a moment as if he did not know who she was.

Then he said, 'God—so that's all it was,' and sat up slowly. He noticed her instantly averted gaze, and his mouth twisted slightly as he pulled the crumpled sheet across his body.

He said, 'I do have these dreams occasionally, but I'm sorry I disturbed you.'

She said, 'It doesn't matter.' She stole a glance at him and saw he was frowning. 'Would it help to talk about the dream?'

He shook his head, and reached for the packet of cigarettes on the table beside the bed.

'I've been promised that they won't last,' he said drily. But then, what does?'

'Do you dream that you're back in Azabia—still running away?' she asked.

'No.' He lit the cigarette and drew on it deeply. 'I'm

back in Azabia, but I'm running nowhere. I'm back in that stinking hole of a jail with the rest of Ben Yusef's "political prisoners".'

She tried to cast her mind back—to remember the order of events. The news of the revolt in Azabia, the deposing and execution of the Sheik, and the arrest of hundreds of his supporters had been shocking enough but then Ben Yusef had ordered all Westerners, especially foreign correspondents, out of his country, saying that he could not guarantee their safety. It had soon become apparent that this was a euphemism for open aggression, and most of the British papers had recalled their correspondents with some speed when they saw the way things were going. But Logan had not returned. He had stayed on, apparently in hiding, to continue to send reports through a short-wave transmitter belonging to a dissident faction which looked on Ben Yusef as a worse choice of leader than the late unlamented Sheik.

She asked, 'When were you captured—how long did you spend in jail?'

He shrugged. 'Six weeks—two months. You begin to lose track of time in these places.' His face hardened. 'They intend you to, of course. There were twelve of us crammed into one cell, with a bucket in the corner. We were given food once a day, if you could call it food, and water, which the guards had spat in, twice.' He saw her face and smiled slightly. 'You shouldn't have asked me, if you didn't want to hear the details, Briony.'

'But I do want to hear,' she protested, sitting down on the edge of the bed and wrapping the folds of her housecoat more closely round her. She had to try and stop her teeth from chattering too noticeably as well, she thought. 'Is that what you dream about—being locked up?'

'Yes,' he said. 'I suppose I must suffer slightly from claustrophobia, although I never realised it until then.

ut there again, I'd never been shut up in a confined space or weeks on end. And then they started coming for the thers. They were all Azabians, except me, and conidered as hostile to the new régime. They used to be aken off for so-called interrogation.' He drew deeply on he cigarette again. 'And then they would be brought ack,' he said.

She watched him in silence, and eventually he began o speak again.

'I think the worst of it was that I didn't know,' he aid. 'Every day when they came for them, you'd swear hey were picking at random, and the thought was lways there in my mind—tomorrow it might be me. nd you can't know, of course, until it happens how ou're going to stand up to that sort of thing—or even if ou are.' He shook his head. 'I couldn't be sure. In the neantime I had to sit against the wall and see every day what they were doing to the others.'

'Oh, Logan!' she whispered.

He looked at her steadily. 'That's what I dream,' he aid. 'I dream that they're coming for me.' His mouth wisted and he stubbed out his cigarette with a sudden iolent movement. 'Not very courageous, is it? But I've een trained all my life to be an observer of the action. 've never found myself actually taking part before. It ertainly stripped away any illusions I might have had bout myself.'

He gave a faint shrug. 'So now you know,' he said. He ave her a closer look and said with a soft groan, 'Oh, od, Briony—no!'

She was crying. She could not help herself, and one low tear after another trickled down her face.

She heard Logan cursing under his breath, then his rms were round her, and her wet face was cradled gainst his chest.

Logan's laconic recounting of his constant nightmare was the trigger for her grief, but as she wept in his arms, her tears dissolved away much of the tension which had possessed her all day, and with it went the bitterness, and the resentment—the hurt which had sustained her, and left her defenceless. His body was warm and under her cheek she could feel the beat of his heart. She turned her head slightly and pressed her lips against his bare skin.

For an instant she felt him grow rigid, and his arms tightened around her to the point of fierceness.

Then he said, 'Go back to your own room, Briony. I don't need your pity or that sort of comfort.'

For a moment she was motionless, then with a little shuddering sigh she got to her feet, straightening the folds of her housecoat, and pushing her tumbled hair back from her tear-stained face. She picked up her candle and walked to the door. She thought she heard him say her name, but it might have been her imagination, and anyway she could not ask him. All she could do was retreat with as much dignity as she had left, because in the morning she would have to face him again.

Her only consolation was that he had read her offering of herself as pity, and not as the hunger for him that she knew it to be. And at least she had not been betrayed into telling him that she loved him.

She blew out the candle and lay staring into the darkness.

CHAPTER SEVEN

'HERE was still no electricity the next day, or the day
fter. In spite of the inconvenience of having to prepare
ıeals on the tiny stove, carefully ekeing out the supply
f gas, Briony could almost be glad that the actual
hysical details of life were becoming a problem. At
:ast it gave her something to think about.

The batteries on Logan's radio had given out as well,
› there were no news transmissions or weather fore-
ısts. In many ways, she thought, staring out of the kit-
ıen window on to the endless whiteness of the fell, it
'as like being in limbo.

Logan shut himself into the parlour first thing each
ıorning and worked steadily throughout the day. Briony
:ntured once over a meal to ask him how it was going,
ıd he returned abruptly that it seemed to be going well.

She found it hard to keep herself occupied in between
eal-getting. She would soon be reduced to the Reverend
[r Gleason, and his attempts to convert the Amazon
ıdians, she thought with a grimace.

Or she could clean the living room properly. It needed
›ing, she decided. She could shake out the mats and
-ush the floor at least.

She was sweeping near the dresser when she suddenly
membered her wedding ring. She knelt down gingerly
ıd peered into the narrow space under the dresser, but
e could see nothing. After a minute she went and
tched the torch from the cellar and knelt down again,
ying awkwardly to send the beam of light where she
anted it.

She nearly jumped out of her skin when Logan sa
just behind her,

'What on earth are you doing? What are you lookir
for?'

She looked round at him, searching for a reasonab
explanation. If she admitted she had lost something, th
he might take it into his head to search himself, and s
didn't want that.

'Woodworm,' she said. 'It's very old, this dresser, a
Aunt Hes wouldn't want anything to happen to it—s
was just checking . . .' Her voice trailed away lamely.

'I see,' Logan said gravely. 'And what were you pla
ning to do? Dazzle them into submission with the torc
or hit them over the head with it when they came out
see what the light was?'

'Very amusing!' Briony scrambled crossly to her fe
brushing off the knees of her jeans. She said sharply, '
isn't lunch time yet, is it?'

'Not yet.' He eyed her flushed averted face. 'What's t
matter?'

'Oh, nothing,' she said on a high note. 'What could p
sibly be the matter? Everything is for the best in this b
of all possible worlds. We're cut off by snowdrifts, there
no electricity, and if this goes on much longer we sh
soon be down to one hot meal a day. Everything's fine!'

Logan's hand shot out and she felt a sharp, stingi
pain across her cheek. She gasped and lifted her hand
her face.

'You hit me!' she accused.

'And not before time.' His voice was harsh. 'Yes, thin
are bad at the moment, and you having a fit of hysteri
will improve nothing.' He glanced about him. 'Nor
this hardly the moment for embarking on spring-clea
ing.'

'Perhaps not,' she said sullenly. 'But at least it keeps me rom thinking.'

His mouth tightened. 'Then don't let me stop you,' he aid. 'I'm going out to do an hour's digging on the track own to the village. If I can clear us a path, it might be an lea to leave the cottage and go down there instead. I preume that the pub is still there? They'd take us in until he roads into the village are cleared.'

She agreed tonelessly, and went on with her selfppointed task. But she did not look for her ring again. Logan came in and found her scrabbling in the dust nce again, he would think she had gone insane.

There was satisfaction in restoring the room to rights, nd dusting and polishing the furniture. She would have ked to have washed the floor, but the precious gas could ot be wasted on heating water for scrubbing floors. She ondered what they would do when it ran out, as it ust surely do in the next day or two. Perhaps they ould contrive some device for cooking on the open fire.

She sighed and pressed a hand to her aching head. The y still looked grey and threatening, she thought as she pened a tin of chopped pork, and heated some baked eans to go with it.

Logan was cold and wet when he came in to eat, and a forbidding mood. She did not ask how much progress e had made, guessing that the snow was deeper than e had anticipated.

When he had finished his meal he went into the parour and began typing. Briony stacked the dishes in the nk, together with the mugs and plates they had used for reakfast, and decided she would do some washing up. he filled a pan with water and put it on the stove to heat p before returning to the living room and the comfort f the fire.

Perhaps she was getting used to the conditions, she

thought, because it had not seemed quite so cold in the kitchen while she was preparing the meal. Or perhaps she had made herself warm with the housework she had done. She was tired after her exertions. Sweeping floors and brushing carpets by hand was quite a different matter from plugging in a vacuum cleaner, she thought sleepily staring at the dancing flames. Her back was aching slightly from bending, and she moved the cushion into a more comfortable position. She mustn't forget the washing up, of course, but surely it could do no harm to close her eyes for a few seconds—only a few seconds, she promised herself.

When she awoke with a start it was growing dark, and she realised the afternoon must be far advanced. In the same moment she remembered the washing up and the pan of water left on the little stove to heat, and jumping to her feet she rushed into the kitchen. The water in the pan was still warm, but the stove itself was cold, its supply of gas finally exhausted while she had slept.

'Oh, no!' she said aloud, almost imploringly as she stared at it. 'No, it can't be!'

She had sat in the other room and simply let it burn away. Like someone in a trance she returned to the living room. The fire had sunk low while she had slept, and she made it up again, kneeling on the rug, her movements mechanical. How—how could she have been so careless, so stupid? she asked herself despairingly. The washing up could have waited anyway. It was far more important that they had something hot to eat and drink. She knew that. What in the world had she been thinking of? It was what Logan would say, she knew. She was simply rehearsing the scene to come. And what was her excuse—that she'd dozed off?

She shook her head. She could always expand on the statement, she supposed. Tell him that she had fallen sleep because she slept so badly at night, alone in her old bedroom, and that she slept badly because thoughts f him, wanting him, filled her mind.

But of course she couldn't say that, because it would reak this weird silent pact of theirs in which they hared a roof, and a few brief words over meals, but othing else. Those moments in his bedroom when she ad wept in his arms might have taken place on a different planet.

She had thought that if she could find her wedding ring nd replace it on her finger, it might be a start towards new understanding between them, but she knew she vas only fooling herself.

Even if she confessed to him that everything she had aid about Christopher had been untrue, and that there vas no other man in her life, it would make no difference.

There was still Karen Wellesley to consider. And oldly, rationally Briony made herself consider her. Made herself think of the final hurt which had sent her unning away from London into this self-imposed exile.

She had waited in vain for Logan to come to the house gain, or at least telephone, but the days had gone by vithout a message, and she was totally bewildered. She vas torn apart too by inward struggle. One side of her ature recoiled in panic at the thought of any kind of nvolvement with him again, warning her that with Logan there could only be eventual heartbreak and disillusionment. But deep within her, a small bud of hope ad begun to blossom, germinated by the knowledge that e had sought her out on his return. So she must ave been on his mind, she thought, with a strange emulous excitement which warred with the panic and eminded her that without Logan she would have nothing at all.

In the end, she had decided that she had to go and see him for herself, and that was what he had been expecting her to do all along. After all, he had made the first move. It was up to her to meet him halfway at least, and it would be better if the meeting took place in a place other than her father's house.

After a lot of soul-searching, she decided to go round to the flat where he used to live. She had no idea if that was where he was still living, but at least the present occupants might have some idea of his whereabouts if not.

She had waited until the coast was clear to make her escape. Between Christopher and her father, she felt she was being kept under constant surveillance. Then she hailed a passing taxi and told the driver to take her to Logan's former address.

All the way there, memories of what had transpired on her last ill-fated visit kept coming back into her mind —Karen Wellesley's gloating face, her half-naked body and worst of all her air of ownership returned to taunt and torment her, so that she was on edge even before the taxi turned into the street.

There was another taxi drawn up at the entrance to the flats, and the occupant was paying off the driver.

Briony registered the newcomer's identity with a feeling of total unreality. It was as if merely by thinking of Karen Wellesley she had summoned her up. As she watched Karen turn away and cross the pavement towards the entrance to the flats, she leaned forward and rapped on the glass to her driver.

'I've changed my mind,' she said, and told him to take her back to the house. As she glanced back she saw Karen Wellesley blow a smiling kiss up at the windows of the flat.

She stared unseeingly out of the window on the drive

ack. Now she knew why Logan had not contacted her gain. Because Karen Wellesley was back in his life gain, celebrating his return. She smothered the sob hich rose in her throat. While she had been sitting at ome, dreaming her romantic dreams, Karen had been ith him, resuming her place in the scheme of things as he had never been away. Perhaps they were even in ve, she told herself. And even if they were not, then ey understood each other. They came from the same orld, had the same goals, held the same values.

She could not compete, and what was more she would ot even try, she told herself proudly. It was that even-g that she had decided to go to Yorkshire. Christopher ad been to dinner, and both he and her father had been essing her to come to some firm decision about the issolution of her marriage.

Feeling as she did, she should have agreed at once, let e tide of their pressure sweep her into a decision. It as her reluctance to begin the process which would ing their strange relationship to its inevitable end that sturbed her.

Logan and she had betrayed each other. What possible ason did she have for hesitation? Questions for which e could find no convincing answers buzzed and seethed her brain, and eventually she had decided to run away. rhaps, she had told herself, a time of solitude was all e needed—a time when no one would be murmuring rsuasive arguments in favour of this or that course of tion. A time to think, and to make a reasoned decision.

Looking back on the way she had tried to rationalise r behaviour, Briony did not know whether to laugh or y. Because if she was honest, all she had done was run vay again.

And what good had her headlong flight done her? Here e was, after all, more unhappy, more confused than she had ever been. But at least she didn't have a decision to make any more. Logan had done that for her.

She wondered why he had not brought Karen with him to the cottage, although she was thankful in the circumstances that he hadn't. The idea of being forced to become an unwilling member of a *ménage à trois* with no means of escape was a repugnant one. She supposed Karen's work had kept her in London. Her life as the *Courier*'s women's editor was a busy one. And Logan had come to the cottage for peace and quiet to work on his manuscript. Perhaps he had felt that Karen's presence would be too much of a distraction.

She got up with sudden resolution and marched across the passage. Normally she knocked before entering when Logan was working, but this time she flung open the door so violently that it banged against the wall.

Logan looked up from his typewriter, his brows lifting in surprise.

'What's the matter?'

'The gas has all gone,' she announced baldly.

He gave a dismayed whistle. 'I thought it would have lasted longer than that.'

'It should have. It would have,' she said. 'Only I used the stove this afternoon, and fell asleep and forgot about it. So all the gas has gone—wasted.' She paused.

'I see.' He gave her a speculative glance. 'Now why don't you tell me what's really eating you?'

'I've told you,' she said off the top of her voice, 'I've just wasted all the bloody gas.'

'So what do you want me to say about that?' he said. 'These things happen? Consider it said.' His tone was openly dismissive and she stiffened.

'I'm so sorry,' she said, poisonously sweet. 'Am I disturbing you with my little domestic problems?'

The aquamarine eyes regarded her levelly. 'You're di

urbing me. I won't add any qualifications.'

His tone was dry, and the implication unmistakable. riony flushed, effectively silenced. She knew that if she ad any sense she would beat a strategic retreat.

Instead she said, gabbling a little, 'I'm sorry I'm in your ray. I've been praying for the thaw as you suggested, ut my prayers don't seem to be answered.'

'Nor mine,' he said pleasantly. 'Besides, a thaw is a ow process. A couple of days' rain would be quicker nd more effective.'

'Is that what you're praying for?'

'If I told you what I was praying for,' he said slowly, 'ou wouldn't believe me. Now go, Briony, and leave me ı peace.'

'Peace?' she echoed almost hysterically. 'What peace is ıere for either of us here?' She made a wild gesture. 'I an't stand being cooped up here like this!'

Logan closed his eyes wearily, as if he was hanging on) his patience with a supreme effort. 'You came here of our own free will,' he said. 'God alone knows why. Is ıat what's needling you, Briony? That for once in your fe there isn't anywhere else to run to? That for once in our spoiled, sheltered existence, you have to stop and ıce up to things? It's certainly time you did.'

'Thank you for the sermon,' she snapped. 'Have you ıy other good advice?'

'Plenty,' he drawled. 'For starters, you'd better go and cquire the knack of cooking on an open fire. That is if ou want any more hot food.'

She took pleasure in slamming the door behind her, ut it was a waste of time. He was typing again before ıe had even got across the passage.

She was blazingly, shiveringly angry, in the mood for ırowing things, or striking out. She'd wanted a con-ontation—wanted to fling in his face her knowledge of

his relationship with Karen Wellesley, but he'd denie
her the opportunity.

Hands balled into impotent fists, she stood staring u
seeingly out of the window.

The way he'd dismissed her—like a schoolgirl who
got above herself—or a domestic servant. How dare
he! she thought hotly. Treating her as if she wasn
worth quarrelling with—and expecting her meekly
come in here and start struggling to cook the supper c
the living room fire. She could have screamed with rage

With sudden resolution she left the living room ar
went upstairs to her room, and began flinging her thin
into her case. Logan had dug the path to the gate and
least part of the way down the track. She would strugg
the rest of the way. If he thought he had her trappe
then he would soon know how mistaken he was!

She put on her sheepskin coat and her gloves, the
crept downstairs. The hinges on the front door creake
a little, and she tensed for a moment, waiting for th
parlour door to open and Logan to demand where sh
was going. But the clatter of the typewriter didn't eve
falter for a moment, and she went out, closing the doo
gently behind her.

He had been sitting with his back to the window, t
catch what little remaining light there was, so with luc
he would not see her going down the path, and she woul
soon be round the bend in the track.

The path was more slippery than she had anticipate
and her boots skidded on the surface. She had to kee
stopping to get her balance, and she was glad there wa
no one around to watch her ungainly progress.

It was easier to walk on the rough surface of the trac
although the path which Logan had cleared was onl
narrow. When it petered out, she paused for a momen
gauging the depth of the snow with some dismay. Sh

wished now that she had not brought her case, but only what she could carry in her pockets.

Cautiously she moved forward on to the snow. She had tucked her cord jeans into the top of her boots, and immediately she was in over her knees. She swore silently. When she had been a child at Branthwaite, snow had been fun to play in. She'd forgotten what hell it was to walk in. She took another tentative step and then another, and gave a little startled cry as she sank up to her thighs. She must have encountered one of the track's many potholes.

She floundered forward, panting as she pushed against the weight of the snow, then came to a standstill to consider her predicament. The first thing she had to do was get rid of her suitcase; she would just have to leave it at the side of the track for the time being. She leaned across the crisp frozen surface of the snow pushing the case away from her with all her strength.

Then she began to move forward again, very slowly, trying desperately to ignore her soaked and freezing legs. She had covered perhaps twenty yards, and already she was exhausted. It wasn't a pothole after all, she realised. It was just that the snow had drifted deeper on the slope of the track. At any moment she could find herself up to her waist.

Her breath sobbing in her throat, she began to push forward again, but the weight of the snow was suddenly too much for her to dislodge and she fell forward ignominiously on to her face. Gasping, she dragged herself back on to her feet. She was wet through now, and her coat felt like a ton weight on her slender shoulders. As she stood motionless, trying to catch her breath and nerve herself for the next stage of the onslaught, she felt a wet drop on her face, then another, and yet another. For a moment she thought it was snowing again, and her heart sank, then as the drops started to increase and gather in momentum, the truth dawned upon her. It was raining.

She stood, stunned in disbelief, watching the dark marks appear on the crisp powdery surface. The wind had risen slightly, and she could hear it sighing mournfully in the trees which bordered the track. Briony could have moaned with it.

She wanted to weep with frustration. If only she had been patient for a little while longer! As it was she was now faced with the choice of either pressing on becoming wetter and more cold and uncomfortable with every laborious step she took or returning to the cottage and having to face Logan.

Gritting her teeth, she took another step, but her searching foot encountered an unknown obstacle, buried deep in the snow, and she fell forward on to her face again. And as she lay there wincing from the pain in her wrenched ankle and wondering dazedly where she was going to find the strength to get up again, she heard Logan call her name. This time she groaned aloud. She had to move—she must, even if she had to crawl on her hands and knees. She couldn't let him come down the track and find her lying there, stricken and helpless.

She struggled to rise, to at least pull herself up on to her hands and knees, but the weight of her soaking clothes were an added encumbrance.

'You damned little fool!' His voice was bleak with rage. 'Will you never learn?'

Briony succumbed unresisting as he lifted her bodily out of the drift. The rain had turned suddenly into a downpour and his tawny hair was plastered to the shape of his head. She wanted suddenly to tell him she was sorry, but the words would not come.

All she managed to say was, 'My case.'

'It will have to stay there,' he said. 'I have enough on ıy hands with you.'

When they reached the path he had dug, she asked in whisper to be put down. Logan hesitated before comying, then set her on her feet very gently. But her ımbed legs would not support her, and she had to cling him.

He said harshly, 'From now on we do this my way,' ıd swung her up into his arms again.

She was amazed to see lights coming from the cottage. ɔgan smiled grimly as he encountered her questioning ok.

'Yes, the power's on again, by some miracle,' he said. erhaps the rain's taken longer to get here than anyhere else.'

He carried her up the path and shouldered his way in rough the front door. The living room fire had been plenished and was roaring up the chimney and he set iony down on the rug in front of it, then disappeared. 'hen he returned some time later he was carrying an mful of towels, and her housecoat. So he'd been to tch her case.

She had been struggling to unfasten her coat, but her ozen fingers would not obey her. She looked at him utely as he came over to her, dropping the towels on the rug. Pushing her hands away, he unfastened her at, and tossed it on to the chair, then tugged her damp veater over her head.

She began to say, 'I can manage now ...' but he told r to shut up in a voice so molten with rage that she ought it was best to do as he said. She stood shivering hile he stripped the sodden clothes from her body and rapped her in a bath towel. Then he began to rub her y. He was brisk, efficient and none too gentle, and adually she felt warmth stealing painfully back into her body. When he had finished towelling her hair h tossed her housecoat to her.

He said, 'Put this on, and don't stir away from tha fire.'

Meekly she complied, sinking down on to the rug and arranging the damp towels on the fender to dry off.

Presently Logan returned with a steaming mug o coffee.

'There's brandy in it,' he said. 'I shall have to re-stocl your aunt's drinks cupboard before we leave.'

Briony murmured something and sipped at the coffee and soon the trembling inside her stopped, and th warmth seemed to penetrate inwards, spreading alon her veins.

She said at last, 'Logan, you're wet too.'

'I'm going to take care of that now,' he said. 'An then I'm going to bring your mattress and bedding dow here. You're going to sleep by the fire tonight. I'm no taking any chances with possible pneumonia.'

When she was alone again, it would have been ver easy to have put her head down and howled in misery Her headlong flight had achieved nothing. Her hea ached and it was difficult even to remember why it ha seemed so important that she should try to get away Everything she did seemed to turn against her, sh thought despairingly.

She heard the mattress bumping down the stairs an jumped up to help Logan with it. He had changed into a pair of dark slacks and a black rollneck sweater an though he looked weary and terrifyingly angry, his at traction still reached out and took her by the throat as i had done the first time she had ever seen him. She foun herself wishing with all her heart that she was that gir again, with the world at her feet, but with the wisdon that the misery of the past year had taught her.

She thought of Karen Wellesley and anger shook her. I should have fought her, she thought. I should have insisted on seeing him that day. My pride might have suffered, but it could have been worth it. I might have fought her and won. After all, it was me that he married. No one can take that away from me.

And no one had. She had relinquished her part in his life, her role, her rights, without a struggle because she had been young and confused and bitter.

And they were still apart at this moment because she'd had no real idea how to regain the ground she had lost. Because they were still, to all intents and purposes, strangers to each other, and therefore wary.

So many times she had sworn she would never forgive him—for the way he had deliberately aroused and humiliated her on their wedding night, for cynically resuming his relationship with his mistress as soon as they had returned to London. So often she had tried to hate him. But it didn't work, she thought. It had never worked because in spite of everything she had never ceased to want him. Even her attempts to revive old memories and old resentments had failed to still the clamour of her senses.

Each time I've run away, she told herself, I've been running from myself as much as I have from him, only I couldn't see it. I didn't want to admit it. And now it's too late.

Too late. The words tolled in her brain like a mourning bell, while the wind-driven rain lashed at the windows in ironic emphasis.

She was suddenly desperate to break the silence which stretched between them. She said, 'The rain—did you know it was going to start?'

He said abruptly, 'I'd wondered. There was that sudden rise in temperature, and the fact that the wind had veered

round to the west. But it seemed too much to hope for.
He gave her a long steady look. 'It's thanks to the rain
that you're here now, and not still lying out in the snow
I came to find you—to tell you it was raining. I looked
all over the house before I could make myself believe
that you'd gone. I didn't think that even you could be
such a fool.'

She said, 'I'm sorry.' And, 'In one way or another
cause you nothing but trouble, don't I?'

He said tightly, 'Well, don't worry about it. If this rain
continues, it shouldn't be for much longer.'

The silence closed in on them again, and she fought i
back.

'What will you do when your book is finished?'

'I haven't decided yet,' he said. 'I have a number o
offers to consider.'

'Will you go on being a foreign correspondent?'

'I don't know.' His voice was impatient. 'That depend
on a lot of things.'

Briony wanted very much to ask just what those
'things' were, and if Karen Wellesley was among them
but her courage failed her, and she sat silent, drinking
her cooling coffee, and listening to the hiss and splatter
of raindrops coming down the chimney and falling on to
the blazing logs in the hearth.

She tried again. 'Is the book going well? Is it doing
what you wanted to do?'

He glanced at her frowning. 'Which was?'

'You said you hoped it would be a kind of exorcism,
she reminded him.

'I don't think I bargained for quite how many demons
there were,' he said drily. 'I think it's going to work up to
a point. And it's taught me a number of things, as well
For instance, I never realised before what a well developed instinct for self-preservation I have. You'd think

that working for your father would have shown me that.'

'And marrying me.' She tried for a smile.

His mouth twisted. 'I think I'd probably categorise that as a self-destructive impulse. But I'd tried to tell myself that at least we'd gone beyond the stage where we could inflict any more damage on each other. Writing the book has told me differently.'

Another blast of rain attacked the window.

'Your salvation,' Logan said bitterly, and dragged the curtains closed with unnecessary violence.

He moved away from the window and stood looking down at her, as she knelt on the rug.

'Another of life's little ironies,' he said. His voice altered, deepened slightly as he quoted, ' "*Western wind, when wilt thou blow The small rain down can rain? Christ if my love were in my arms And I in my bed again.*" ' His face was bitter and brooding as he looked at her. 'Only for us the reverse is true, isn't it, Briony? The western wind is going to blow you away from me—from my arms, from my bed, from my life. I didn't believe it at first, when the rain started. I'd thought that I had at least two more days to try and unravel this desperate mess we were in.'

He dropped to his knees beside her, cupping her face between his hands and turning her towards him.

'And suddenly there's no time any more,' he said, and there was a note in his voice which triggered off answering tremors in her innermost being. 'I've tried to fight it, Briony. I've reminded myself a hundred times that you don't belong to me. That you never did in any real sense, and that now there's someone else in your life. But it's no good. I can't fight any more.'

His hands reached round, caressing the nape of her neck, lifting the fall of copper hair clear of it, letting it slide through his fingers like silk.

'It wasn't just self-preservation which kept me running in Azabia,' he said. 'I was always on the move, one step ahead of Ben Yusef's thugs, passed from hand to hand, from house to house by people who were even more frightened than I was. I didn't sleep much, but I used to have this dream. You were with me, Briony,'—his hands were unutterably gentle as they loosened the belt of her housecoat, and slid it from her shoulders—'and your hair was spread across my pillow. Even when I was awake I could still see you. I swore then that if I got clear and came back to the United Kingdom, I'd make that dream into reality.'

She tried to say something past the tightness in her throat, but he laid a finger on her lips as if he was forbidding her to speak, and then he began to touch her, lightly and delicately as if she were the most fragile porcelain, and he a blind man whose only source of knowledge was through his fingertips, and speech was not only impossible suddenly, but unnecessary.

His voice was almost reflective, but there was a ragged note in it which made Briony realise how tenuous a thing his apparent self-control was.

He said, 'But it all went sour on me when I did get back. For one thing I had to see you in your father's house. I didn't dare ask you to meet me somewhere else in case you refused. I needed to see you so badly—and there you were, standing on the stairs, all dressed up and very definitely had somewhere to go. And I realised suddenly that you'd made a whole new life for yourself which I had no part in, and it would be better if I went. I hung around for days on end, hoping that you'd get in touch, and eventually London became intolerable, and I decided to come here.' He drew a long breath and she was aware that he was trembling. 'And there you were.' His voice was suddenly harsh. 'And here you are.'

His mouth burned on her, and the flame he lit was all-ncompassing and merciless, and there was no drawing ack for either of them as they were engulfed. Her parted ps returned his kisses with an eagerness she did not ven pretend to conceal. The time for pretence was long ast, and she heard herself whimpering with delight as ie long, languorous passage of his hands and mouth over er body aroused her almost to madness. And then the inguor changed to urgency as he pushed her back on to ie rough material of the mattress and his body covered ers.

She cried out once, half in pain and half in surprise at ie unfamiliarity of this new and ultimate intimacy, then istinct took over and the mystery disappeared for ever, be replaced by the certainty of this giving and taking hich seemed at once endless and yet, with her last oherent thought before she was claimed and consumed y pleasure, over much too soon.

'Much too soon,' she murmured later, lying in Logan's ms in the drowsy aftermath of that shattering cul-iination, and heard him laugh deep in his throat.

'You're forgetting.' He put his lips hungrily to the ulse in her throat, then feathered a long line of kisses own to her breast. 'We have the whole night ahead of s.'

CHAPTER EIGHT

RIONY awoke the next morning to a feeling of well-eing which was not immediately dissipated by the ealisation that she was alone. She wriggled down into er covering of blankets and let her mind roam back

over the preceding night, while her physical being as-
similated certain facts, the first of which was that sh
ached rather pleasantly.

There was a new sensuality in the reminiscent smil
which curled round the swollen softness of her mouth, a
she remembered the heights and the depths of passio
which Logan had taught her. And yet nothing had seeme
sufficient to assuage their fierce and mutual need.

She turned her head, listening for sounds of movemen
in the kitchen, but all was silent. Yet he couldn't be fa
away because the fire had been made up and the heart
swept at some time.

She got up, draping a blanket round her body like
toga, and wandered over to the window. It was still raining, although the wind had dropped, and the unceasin
monotonous torrent had transformed the pristine un-
trodden whiteness of the snow into unappealing slush.

Briony wrinkled her nose and turned away. Sh
dropped her covering blanket on to the tangled cover
and stretched luxuriously in the warmth from the fire
before reaching for her housecoat. Then she went int
the kitchen and put the kettle on to make herself som
coffee. She heard an anxious mewing at the back door
and when she opened it, the bedraggled cat shot past he
into the living room. Briony chuckled. The cat had hel
aloof, during the snow, occupying an empty box in th
woodshed. Now the rain had forced it to seek shelter an
human companionship again. Cats didn't mind bein
cold, but they hated being wet, she thought, as sh
opened a tin of corned beef and chopped some on to
saucer for it. She carried the saucer through to the living room and set it down on the rug, where the cat wa
grooming itself.

'You'll get no better service anywhere,' she assured it

as it turned surprised green eyes upon her, and she laughed out loud in irrepressible jubilation.

She knelt down and began to fold the sheets and blankets which Logan had brought down the night before. Tonight, she thought, they would sleep together in the bed upstairs where their marriage should have begun all those months before, and the wheel would come full circle.

She bent and pressed her lips to the pillow they had shared, then snatched it up, hugging it almost fiercely to her breasts. It's all right, she told herself. Everything is going to be all right—particularly when she solved the growing mystery of where Logan had got to.

On her way upstairs with the bedding, she paused to glance in at the parlour door. The typewriter stood in the centre of the table with the unfinished page still held in its rollers, and she could not explain the curious feeling of relief that she experienced on still seeing it there.

She tried to rally herself, to shake off the slight feeling of depression that was beginning to invade her. The euphoria of her first waking moments had worn off completely by now.

On an impulse, she went into the bathroom and ran herself a steaming tub. There was some French bath essence belonging to Aunt Hes in the bathroom cupboard and she splashed it generously into the water. She hoped a long hot soak would cheer her up and help banish some of her apprehensions, but she could not relax. She kept listening for the sound of Logan's return, and asking herself where he had gone. He must have gone down to the village, she reasoned, wondering what state the track was in, probably to try and get hold of some fresh bread and milk. But if Kirkby Scar itself had been cut off, would there have been any deliveries? She sighed in perplexity, submerging herself up to the chin in the warmth of the water.

She was humming a little tune as she went into the bedroom. After some thought she decided against the various pairs of jeans she had been wearing over the past few days, and put on a calf-length russet velvet skirt with a matching shirt top. She brushed her hair until it crackled with electricity and let it hang loose on her shoulders. She pulled a little face at the shadows under her eyes, then smiled as she remembered the reason for them.

She hummed again as she ran downstairs and turned into the living room, then paused in astonishment as her eyes took in Logan's coat, draped across the back of a chair to dry. So he'd come back, then—without a word. She stood, conscious of a sudden chill, and heard the sound of the typewriter coming from the parlour.

She turned slowly and went across the passage. The door was closed, and she opened it without knocking and went in.

He was sitting, his head bent, typing furiously, all his attention, all his concentration on the words appearing on the page in front of him.

Briony said his name, and knew that he had heard her because she saw him stiffen slightly, but he did not look up at once, and she stood there in front of him vulnerable and defenceless.

At last he did look at her and his eyes were cool and remote. She waited breathlessly for him to get up and come round the table to her. Her mouth was dry, and her inside was churning, and only his arms around her would give her the peace and reassurance she wanted.

He said, 'Good morning. The track to the village is just about negotiable, you'll be pleased to hear. I called at the garage while I was down there and they're sending someone to have a look at your car.'

Utterly bewildered, she said, 'Thank you. I—I guessed you'd gone to the village. Did you get any bread?'

He shook his head. 'We'll have to make do with what food we have left for the short time remaining.'

'Short time?' she echoed, staring at him. 'I don't understand.'

Logan shrugged. 'I think it's best for us to get out of here while the going's good,' he said. 'In the village, they're talking about flooding further down the valley already. We don't want the weather to trap us here again.'

She tried to smile. 'I wouldn't mind.'

'I think you would in time. Anyway, the question loesn't arise. I've booked myself a room at the Black Bull for tonight.'

'Don't you mean you've booked *us* a room?'

'If I'd meant that,' he said wearily, 'I'd have said it. 've booked myself a room. You'll be long gone by toight.' She saw his mouth tighten. 'I've telephoned your ather. He's coming for you.'

There was a silence, then Briony said helplessly, 'I lon't believe you. Why should you...? I thought—last ight...'

'Last night was last night,' he said. 'It is now the cold ight of day, and time we started seeing things in their ight perspective.' His voice was cool, almost laconic.

She took a step forward. 'You're joking—you must be! lease don't tease me, Logan, it's not kind.'

'I'm quite serious,' he said. 'And I'm being much kinder han you think. Nothing has really changed, you know. Ve're still the same people. All we've really learned is ow to please each other in bed.'

'That isn't all,' she said past the hard lump in her throat. 'Or it isn't for me at least. I love you, Logan.'

He said quietly, 'Briony, you're just making this harder on both of us. What you're really saying is that you like making love with me. But I'm the only lover you've ever had, so how can you know that you won't enjoy what we had together just as much or more with someone else?'

'I don't want anyone else,' she said tonelessly.

'Perhaps not at this moment.' There was no amusement in his faint smile. 'I wouldn't feel very flattered if you did. But you have a life to make for yourself, and some day soon there'll be another man in that life.' He paused. 'This man you're practically engaged to—this Christopher—what about him?'

'He doesn't mean a thing to me.' She was practically wringing her hands. 'I—I only told you he did because I was frightened of you, of how you could make me feel.'

'Well, you clearly mean a great deal to him,' Logan said drily. 'He's on his way here too, with your father.'

'Oh, no!' Briony was aghast. 'I don't want him here. I don't want either of them.' She stared at him. 'Why did you do this?'

'Because it occurred to me that your father would probably be worried out of his mind about you. You are his only child, after all, and I must give him credit for possessing some normal feelings.'

'You told him that we'd been here—together?'

'I didn't tell him about last night, if that's what you mean. I merely said that we'd both turned up here and been cut off by the snow ever since.'

'What did he say?'

'Let's just say his reaction was—predictable.' Logan gave a slight shrug. 'Which is one of the reasons I took the room at the Black Bull.'

'Scared, Logan?' she asked evenly. A bright spot of
olour burned in each of her pale cheeks.

'No.' His mouth twisted contemptuously. 'I merely
ought it would be less hassle for you if I was out of the
ay.'

'Oh, you're all consideration.' She wanted to scream
ut loud, and throw herself down and drum her heels, but
stead she had to stand there in front of the table like
unsuccessful candidate at an interview and listen to
m calmly and uncaringly smashing every dream she
ossessed. 'You were gone quite a long time. Was—was
y father the only person you telephoned?'

'No. Does it matter?'

'It could explain a good deal,' she said, and laughed
ther wildly. 'You were so quick to reassure me that
ere would be other men in my life, that it almost never
curred to me that the obverse will also be true. That
ere'll be other women in yours.' She paused. 'Well? I
otice that you don't deny it.'

'If ever I decide to become a monk,' he said softly, 'I'll
ter a monastery.'

She said in a voice she didn't recognise, 'Did you phone
aren Wellesley?'

Logan's head lifted sharply and he looked at her for a
ng moment. When he spoke, his voice seemed to come
om a far distance. He said, 'Yes.'

ie house seemed empty and weird after he had gone.
iony sat listlessly by the living room fire and listened
the sound of the rain, which was falling more heavily
an ever. The view from every window was the same—
grey sodden morass, interspersed with patches of melt-
g snow, reflecting the dull hue of the heavy sky.

She felt drained and empty, and cold to the bone. It
as impossible to believe that only a few hours before

she and Logan had been here together on that makeshif bed in front of the fire. Incredible to remember the pas sion and the laughter and the tenderness, and the swif fierce ascent to passion again. Her throat closed at th memory of it.

She had given Logan everything she had to give. Sh had believed in her naïvety that generosity would mak up for her lack of experience, and she had been totall generous, her surrender complete. Yet it had not bee enough. She had seen it as the beginning of a real rel tionship. She had thought he felt the same. She'd been s sure ...

She gave a long, quivering sigh. Now she was sure c nothing, least of all of her own feelings. Emotionally, sh felt bruised, as she had done when she received the repo of his death. Perhaps the bruises would fade in time, c at least not hurt quite as much.

Perhaps there would even come a time when she woul be able to think of him with Karen Wellesley and nc know the pain which was tearing her apart at th moment.

She couldn't think about that now. She couldn't allo herself to think because it was very important that sh be calm and self-controlled when her father and Chri topher arrived. For her pride's sake, she had to have he dignity intact, and not let them find her tear-stained an red-eyed.

She would follow the lead Logan had already giver she thought dully, and let them think that they had bee reluctant sharers of the same roof and nothing more.

Suddenly during the course of the long afternoon sh remembered her wedding ring again, and her abortiv attempt to retrieve it from beneath the dresser. This tim she would find it, she vowed. At least she would hav something of Logan to remember.

She got the torch, and fetched a broom from the kitchen and lay full length on the floor. But all she unearthed with her frantically prodding broom handle was dust and a few disgruntled spiders. The ring seemed to have vanished completely, probably down some unseen crack in the floor, she thought despondently as she got slowly to her feet. Even the smallest memento of her brief and transitory happiness was to be denied her, it seemed.

She had resumed her seat by the fire when she realised that there were people coming up the path. She could hear masculine voices, and knew with a sinking heart that her father had arrived.

He was very angry, she saw as she opened the door in answer to his thunderous knock, but keeping it under control. Christopher standing behind him, his elegant overcoat collar turned up against the all-pervading damp, looked plain miserable.

'And what is the meaning of this?' Sir Charles demanded tautly as he went into the living room. 'Do you realise what you've made me suffer in the past week, you thoughtless, irresponsible child?'

Christopher reached for her hand. 'Darling, why didn't you tell us where you were going?'

'Because I didn't want you to follow me,' she said quietly, removing her fingers from his grasp.

'Isn't the real reason because you had a rendezvous with that Adair man?' Sir Charles barked.

'No,' she said calmly. 'My arrival here was as unpleasant a shock to Logan as his was to me. In the circumstances, he was the last person I wanted to see. However,' her voice wavered slightly, 'we do seem to have reached an agreement that we do not—agree, and that's what you wanted to happen, wasn't it?'

'I should have thought you could have reached the same agreement in London,' Sir Charles muttered. 'Why in the world you had to come to the back of beyond——' He gave the comfortable living room a comprehensive glance of utter dislike. 'How many rooms are there in the place?'

'Enough,' Briony said sweetly, thanking heaven that Logan had replaced the mattress and bedding upstairs in the front room. 'Would you like to go upstairs and have a look at the sleeping arrangements?'

'Of course not,' Christopher interposed hastily. 'We trust you, darling. But it must have been an awful experience for you—awkward, embarrassing.'

'Very,' she said. She turned to her father. 'I don't know what arrangements you've made for getting back to Town, but I ought to warn you that my car is being looked over in the local garage. It may just be a question of re-charging the battery, but I can't be sure.'

'Christopher will bring your car back,' Sir Charles said with an impatient wave of his hand. 'One of the company cars and a chauffeur is waiting for us at the village inn. Are your things packed? I'd like to start back as soon as possible.'

She put on her coat while Christopher went up and fetched her case. As they walked down the path, picking their way between deep pools of slush, Briony wanted to turn and look at the cottage, but she wouldn't allow herself to do so. She could not rely on maintaining her cool façade if she did, she knew.

There were still patches of deep snow on the track, and Briony skirted them with care. Sir Charles' temper was not improved by a second encounter with the slippery hazardous surface, while Christopher's face took on a martyred expression as more and more splashes accumulated on his elegant City clothes.

The bar at the Black Bull wasn't open yet, so Sir Charles strode into the lounge demanding a tray of tea ınd sandwiches to be brought to them. Christopher was lispatched to the garage to find out about Briony's car, nd returned presently looking even more wet and nartyred to say that he'd told them to install a new batery as they were in a hurry.

Briony found herself watching him as she forced herelf to sip some tea and eat one of the sandwiches. He vas pleasant enough, she supposed, but far too much of yes-man for her father—as indeed were most of the nen she had encountered—with one exception, she hought.

There was no sign of Logan anywhere, and she had to e glad of it, because the prospect of the kind of scene er father was quite capable of creating in his present nood filled her with trepidation. She was too tired and o unhappy to cope with quarrelling and angry voices. he wondered if Logan knew they were downstairs, and hought it was quite likely. Sir Charles' personality ended to fill most places, and in a small place like the lack Bull he was almost overwhelming.

She followed her father out into the street and stood vaiting in the pub doorway while the chauffeur brought he car up to where they were standing.

'You can follow us in Briony's car, Christopher,' Sir harles barked authoritatively. 'And keep your foot own if you don't want to be left behind.'

It was comfortable in the back of the limousine, she ad to admit, and it was pleasant having a cushion laced behind her back and a rug tucked over her knees o keep out non-existent draughts. She leaned back and losed her eyes, and was asleep even before the car had dged forward out of the village street on the journey outh.

When she woke they were somewhere on the motorvay. Her father had been dozing too, and the rest seemed to have improved his temper. Either that or the prospect of finding himself on the way back to his own familiar territory, with a situation that he could control once more, she thought cynically.

He made sure the glass partition between driver and passengers was securely closed before he said, 'It's a good thing Christopher's an easygoing man, my dear.' He chuckled slightly with a satisfied air. 'I don't think I'd have been pleased in his position to learn that you were holed up in the wilds of Yorkshire with another man.'

'Logan can hardly be described as another man,' she said coldly. 'He is still my husband, if only legally. And what precisely is Christopher's "position", as you put it?'

'Why—er——' Sir Charles looked momentarily disconcerted. 'As your future husband ...'

She shook her head decisively. 'Oh, no, Father. I haven't made one mistake only to rush headlong into another. I'm sorry if Christopher has—expectations of me, but I can promise you that they'll never be fulfilled.'

'I see.' Sir Charles frowned. 'Well, I wouldn't wish to influence your decision, my dear child.'

In other words, she supplied silently, he has also had second thoughts about Christopher as a future son-in-law for some reason. Well, hurrah for the reason, whatever it is.

Her father was looking at his watch and making vaguely irritable noises.

'A drive of this length is far too much in one day,' he declared. 'It would have been much better to have spent the night somewhere.'

'Then why don't we?' Briony queried indifferently.

'Because I have a full day of meetings tomorrow,' Sir Charles said crossly. 'Not to mention this question of appointing the new women's editor to the *Courier*.' He sighed. 'Mackenzie wants to make it an internal promotion, but I would like to bring over Helen Mortimer from the *Echo*. I feel that she has the right approach and would ...'

'Just a minute,' Briony cut across him. 'Is—is Karen Wellesley leaving the *Courier*?'

'Yes,' said Sir Charles. 'And damned inconvenient it is just at the moment. But her husband has just been appointed to the Paris office, and naturally she wants to be with him.'

'Her husband?' Briony echoed weakly.

'Yes. They were married about a month back. Very quiet affair. The first the board knew of it was when she handed her notice in.'

'Who did she marry?'

'Fellow called Tony Ericson—in foreign news.'

Briony was stunned into silence by the news. Karen was married—and to Logan's former flatmate! Karen, in fact, had already been married when she had seen her, as she thought, going to meet Logan at the flat.

Her father said, 'What in the world's the matter? You've gone as white as a sheet.'

'It's very stuffy in here,' she managed. 'Could we have the window slightly open, do you suppose?'

The air was cool and damp on her face as she sat, trying desperately to think, to make sense of it all. Karen married! Then what possible role could Logan still play in her life, particularly in view of the fact that she would soon be off to Paris anyway? Briony couldn't believe that Logan wouldn't know of her marriage, especially as Tony and he had been friends, so why hadn't he told her about it? Why had he let her think that morning that he and Karen were still involved?

Her brain was still whirling as they pulled in at the next service station for petrol. Briony climbed out of the upholstered luxury of the limousine to stretch her legs, just as Christopher pulled in behind them. She walked over to him and he wound down the window.

'How's the car running?' she asked.

'All right,' he said rather sulkily. 'I can't get used to the gearbox yet, and it's smaller than I'm used to driving.'

'Poor Christopher,' she said mockingly. 'Want to let me drive? I've discovered I don't make a very good passenger.'

He stared at her in slight dismay. 'But your father . . .'

'Oh, he won't mind,' she said airily. 'Besides, you'll be with me to make sure I keep on the straight and narrow—in this case the fast lane to London.'

'I suppose so,' he said warily. 'I'd better just see what he says.'

'You do that,' she agreed.

Sir Charles made little fuss at the idea of her changing cars. He had, he said, some papers in his briefcase which he wanted to go over, and he would only be poor company for her.

It was good to be back behind the wheel again, and to have something to concentrate on, to take her mind off all the questions which were buzzing unanswered in her brain.

She drove steadily, keeping her father's tail-lights always in view. Christopher, beside her, looked hunched and rather miserable as if he too wished he had some papers to bury himself in. Briony thought, Maybe he knows that he's out of favour. And wondered why.

At last she asked, 'Was Daddy terribly angry when Logan phoned and told him where I was?'

'Angry,' Christopher said fervently, 'wasn't the word for it.' He gave her a sidelong glance. 'I always knew he disliked your—your husband, but I don't think I realised quite how much until this morning.'

'It took me quite a time to realise too,' she said drily, remembering the file of cuttings hidden in the desk drawer, and the woman paid to divide and destroy. If he'd done it once, she thought, he could do it again. She tried to make her voice casual. 'He's so impatient, of course. He must have known that the marriage wouldn't work, but that didn't stop him trying a few dirty tricks to speed the process along, as it were.' She gave him a quick glance. 'I hope I'm not shocking you.'

'Not at all,' he laughed awkwardly. 'They say, don't they, that all's fair in love and war? And it's certainly war between Logan and your father.'

'Yes.' It was starting to rain again, and she switched on the windscreen wipers. 'They quarrelled, then?'

'That's putting it mildly.' Christopher sighed. 'I thought at first your father was going to have an apoplectic fit. He kept shouting "I won't have it, do you hear? You get out of her life, and you stay out!"' He shook his head. 'Odd, really. I suppose your—husband can't have made it clear to him that the marriage was over, or he wouldn't ...' He stopped suddenly.

'He wouldn't what?' Briony pressed gently.

'Wouldn't have insulted him as he did, I suppose,' Christopher said after a pause.

He was aware that he was being indiscreet, and was retreating into silence she realised. Her brain worked madly.

She said with a light laugh, 'I should think Logan's quite used to Daddy's insults.' She managed a slight yawn. 'Don't tell me he tried to buy him off again?'

'Well, yes.' Christopher looked thoroughly taken aback. 'You mean it's happened before?'

'In a way.' The steering wheel was beginning to feel slippery in her hands. She said smilingly, 'It would serve Daddy right if Logan took the money.'

'Oh, but he didn't,' Christopher assured her hastily. 'I don't know what he said, but I think it must have been equally insulting, because Sir Charles went crimson, and couldn't speak for a moment or two. When he started again, the air was blue, I can tell you. He said the reason your husband wouldn't take the money he offered was because he expected to get far more than that when he—Sir Charles that is—died, you being his heiress. Hey!' He grabbed at the steering wheel in alarm. 'Mind that lorry!'

'I saw it,' she said through stiff lips. 'What else did he say?'

'Not much.' Christopher was clearly uncomfortable. 'Look here, Briony, I shouldn't even have told you this much.'

'But you have,' she said. 'And now you can tell me the rest of this charming one-sided conversation.'

'There was nothing charming about it,' he said sullenly. 'Your father told your husband that unless he got out of your life for good, he would cut you out of his will—leave you entirely penniless. He said, "She's enjoyed being a rich man's daughter. Let's see how long she can stand being a poor man's wife. And you haven't even got a job any more."' He stopped and looked at her stricken face. 'Well, you did ask me,' he said defensively.

'What happened then?' She moistened her dry lips with her tongue.

Christopher thought for a moment. 'Not a great deal,' he said at last. 'Your father began to look pleased, and then he put the phone down, and he was smiling. "Well, I've made sure that we've seen the last of him," he said.' He sighed. 'I'm afraid I was shocked, and I showed it.'

Shocked, Briony thought, or anxious in case Sir Charles was setting a precedent for the treatment of sons-in-law unfortunate enough to arouse his displeasure? But it didn't matter. All that mattered was that she knew the truth. She set her indicator going and drew on to the hard shoulder.

'What's the matter?' Christopher demanded. 'Is something wrong with the engine?'

'The engine's fine,' she said. 'This is where you get out, Christopher, I'm afraid. There's an exit just ahead, and I'm going back to Yorkshire while I've still got time. Don't worry. Daddy will soon notice that we're not behind him and come back to have a look. Or you can hitch-hike if you prefer not to face him just yet. I'll tell you something—I bet Logan won't be the only one without a job very soon.' She leaned across him and opened the passenger door, as he seemed paralysed with shock. 'Out,' she said mercilessly.

It was nearly closing time when her car drew up in front of the Black Bull. She switched off the engine and ran into the foyer. One glance into the crowded bar told her that Logan was not there, and the surprised girl who came in answer to her imperative ring on the brass bell on the reception desk told her that Mr Adair had decided not to stay after all, and had left early that evening.

'Where did he go, do you know?' Briony demanded urgently, but the receptionist couldn't say.

Briony walked back into the dark street. The rain had eased somewhat, and a scatter of stars was dimly visible between the bulk of the slowly moving clouds. Logan, she supposed, would also be on his way to London by now; she had probably passed him on her mad dash here. She stiffened suddenly as a thought struck her. The next moment she was running down the village street.

The track was worse than ever in the darkness, and she was splashed from head to foot with slush and dirty water by the time she reached the cottage gate. She leaned on the gate for a moment to catch her breath, straining her eyes towards the living room window, wondering if she was just imagining that the curtains were drawn and a faint chink of light peeping from between them.

She opened the gate and stumbled up the path. The front door wasn't locked and a great breath of relief escaped from her as she flung herself across the threshold.

She opened the living room door and went in. Logan was sitting by the fire, his head buried in his hands. At the sound of her entrance he looked up sharply, his brows snapping together in disbelief as he looked at her.

He demanded, 'What the hell are you doing here? I thought you'd be in London by now.'

'I bet you did.' She slipped off her jacket and let it fall to the floor. She said simply, 'Oh, darling, why didn't you ask me if I'd rather be a rich man's daughter than a poor man's wife?'

She took one step, and she was in his arms, and he was kissing her as he'd kissed her the previous night, with passion and tenderness—and love. She knew it now with a deep and radiant certainty, and her heart sang joyously as she clung to him.

Presently he lifted her into his arms and sat with her by the fire, holding her close against him as if he would never let her go.

He said, 'I've got something for you.'

Briony looked down wonderingly at the little circle of gold he was holding out to her.

'My ring!' she exclaimed. 'Where did you find it?'

'Under the dresser first thing this morning. I was curious to know what you'd been looking for the other day, so I poked about a little bit. It had rolled almost to the back,' he said, sliding it on to her finger. 'I intended to give it to you when you woke up. Then I spoke to your father, and everything changed.'

'Why didn't you tell me that he'd tried to bribe you to

eave me and then threatened to cut me out of his will nstead?' She put a caressing hand against his cheek.

'I think I was afraid to,' he said after a pause. 'In a vay, I felt your father had a point, even though I didn't ke the way in which he expressed it. You would be giv- ng up a great deal if you stayed with me. I can't guaran- ee the book will be a success, and I have no other job at he moment. Besides, the thing between us was so new, o fragile, I didn't know whether it would be strong nough to withstand an open breach with your father.'

'You didn't trust me.' She wound her fingers in his hair nd tugged at it.

'You didn't trust *me*.' He kissed her parted lips linger- ngly. 'Why did you drag poor Karen into the conversa- ion? Though I must admit it was useful, as I was trying o drive you away. And I had phoned her, as it happened, o ask if I could take over the tenancy of the flat again nce she'd departed to join Tony.'

'So that's why she was on her way there that day,' said riony, thinking aloud, and blushed fierily when she met is questioning glance. 'It doesn't matter,' she mumbled.

'I think it does,' he said gravely. 'All right, Karen and I vere—involved for a time, but it had finished even be- ore I started going out with you. What made you think he was still part of my life?'

'She did,' Briony said unhappily. 'I went round to see ou after I discovered that my father had bribed Marina Chapman—oh! Of course, you didn't know about that.'

'I guessed,' he said. 'Her appearance on the scene was ıst too damned convenient, and the effect it would have n you had been gauged by someone who knew you very vell. But go on. You came round to see me—when and vhy?'

'It wasn't very long after we'd got back from here,' he said. 'Perhaps a fortnight or less. I wanted to tell you that I was sorry for the hysterical way I'd behaved. I wanted to tell you what my father had done, and ask if we could begin again. But Karen answered the door. She —she wasn't dressed, and she said—things which made me think you were sleeping with her again. She wouldn't let me see you, or talk to you.'

'She couldn't,' Logan said drily. 'I was down in Cornwall for most of the fortnight that we should have been on our honeymoon. I was pretty broken up when I got back to the flat, and Tony saw it. I couldn't go into work because that would have set tongues wagging, and I was drinking too much, so Tony sent me down to stay with a cousin of his who runs a small hotel near Fowey. I walked a lot, and went out in their boat, and gradually I began to get my head together again.' He took her hand and lifted it to his lips. 'You weren't the only one who had things to apologise for, you know. I loathed myself for the way I'd treated you that night. You were so sweet, so responsive—God!' He shook his head. 'The hardest thing I ever did was turn away from you.' His mouth found hers. 'Almost as hard as sending you away today,' he murmured against her lips.

'But why was Karen at the flat?' Briony persisted when she was allowed to speak again. 'And why did she pretend there was still something between you?'

Logan shrugged. 'She was at the flat because she'd asked if she could borrow it as Tony was abroad and I was away while her own was being redecorated. As for why she said what she did'—he was silent for a moment—'perhaps, for a while, it was more finished for me than it was for her. She didn't like you, and perhaps she saw a chance to get back at you.' He pulled her close to him. 'Anyway, she's married to Tony now and they're blissfully happy, so let sleeping dogs lie.' His exploring hand found the soft curve of her breast, and lingered. 'And what about you, Mrs Adair? Are you going to make me blissfully happy?'

Briony was oddly shy and a little breathless as he began to unfasten the buttons on the velvet shirt.

'Logan, what will we do if my father comes chasing me?'

'Exactly what we're doing now.' He eased the velvet from her shoulders and let it drop to the floor. 'God, but you're lovely,' he said huskily. 'And the imminent arrival of all the fathers in the world isn't going to make the slightest difference to my plans for the next few hours. I love you, Briony, and this is going to be the honeymoon we never had. Sure you don't want to run away again while you still have the chance?'

'I stopped running a long time ago,' she whispered, sliding her arms round his neck and drawing him down to her.

His kiss was warm and possessive and increasingly urgent, ending only as he rose to his feet, still holding her cradled against him. His eyes were tender as he smiled down into her flushed face.

'You'll never be rid of me, then,' he said softly, and in his voice Briony heard the promise of future joys as yet undreamed of.

The Mills & Boon Rose is the Rose of Romance

Every month there are ten new titles to choose from — ten new stories about people falling in love, people you want to read about, people in exciting, far-away places. Choose Mills & Boon. It's your way of relaxing.

June's titles are:

JACINTHA POINT *by Elizabeth Graham*
To save her father, Laurel had been forced to marry the masterful Diego Ramirez, a man she did not know and certainly did not love.

FUGITIVE WIFE *by Sara Craven*
Briony had no doubts about her love for Logan Adair. Yet their marriage had been nothing but a farce from the very beginning.

A FROZEN FIRE *by Charlotte Lamb*
What would happen to Helen's sense of duty to her blatantly unfaithful husband now that Mark Eliot had come into her life?

TRADER'S CAY *by Rebecca Stratton*
There was bound to be tension between Francesca and Antonio Morales, but it was Francesca's relationship with his son Andrés that caused the real trouble between the two of them . . .

KISS OF A TYRANT *by Margaret Pargeter*
When Stacy Weldon first met Sloan Maddison he seemed decidedly antagonistic to her; yet why should he concern himself over the job his mother had offered her?

THE LAIRD OF LOCHARRUN *by Anne Hampson*
What had the formidable Craig Lamond been told about Lorna to make him so hostile to her?

NO WAY OUT *by Jane Donnelly*
Lucy's beloved twin sister had pretended to Daniel Stewart that she was in fact Lucy, and it shouldn't have been difficult for Lucy to deceive him in her turn. But . . .

THE ARRANGED MARRIAGE *by Flora Kidd*
Roselle's marriage to Léon Chauvigny had never been a real one. Now the time had come to end it once and for all. Or had it?

OUTBACK RUNAWAY *by Dorothy Cork*
Running away from the heartbreak of a disastrous love affair, all Dale found was Trelawney Saber, with a bracingly unsympathetic attitude to her troubles!

VALLEY OF THE HAWK *by Margaret Mayo*
Damon Courtney jumped to all the wrong conclusions about Corrie – and turned her life upside down in the process!

If you have difficulty in obtaining any of these books from your local paperback retailer, write to:

Mills & Boon Reader Service
P.O. Box 236, Thornton Road, Croydon, Surrey, CR9 3RU.